IT'S FINALLY SUNNY

J.L. FICKLING

ISBN:
ISBN-13: 978-0692876909
ISBN-10: 0692876901

DEDICATION

To my Husband… Thanks for putting up with my bullshit. Till the wheels fall off baby.

CONTENTS

1

"1st Class trauma, 20-year-old black female, GSW entry right side of chest through and through, extensive blood loss, BT 36.1, BP 85/55, RR 4 per minute, HR 55 per minute. She's going to code get the crash carts ready STAT!"

The trauma center at the University of Michigan Hospital received the Trauma Activation System call for Sunny. She was being transported by the survival flight helicopter due to her grave condition. Sunny laid strapped to the gurney, fading in and out of consciousness. She could hear the loud whipping noise of the helicopter blades propelling ferociously against the wind. Sunny felt cold, numb and afraid. She tried to speak but no words could flow from her mouth. She tried to sit up but her body was frozen stiff; unable to move even an inch. "Sunny! Sunny! Stay with us honey! We're almost at the hospital. You fight got damnit. Keep fighting Sunny! Stay with us darling!" The survival flight nurse shouts into Sunny's ear to ensure she hears him over the loud noise of the helicopter and her loss of consciousness. The chopper finally lands and the rescue team whisks Sunny away to the emergency room.

"CODE BLUE! ADULT CODE BLUE UH ER ROOM 727!" Sunny has flat lined. She is clinically dead. The medical team is scrambling around the room ripping open the crash cart and medical supplies. The emergency resident jumps on top of Sunny's stretcher and performs chest compressions as the defibrillator charges. "CLEAR!" *ZAP* Electrical currents are sent to Sunny's heart in hopes of making it beat again. Sunny doesn't have a pulse. The doctor punches Sunny's chest as if his fist were a gavel. He proceeds with chest compressions. "CLEAR!" The medical team stares intently at the heart monitor in silence... "Got damnit baby girl. Come on back Sunny!" The resident doctor yells. "Don't call it yet. Crank up the Defib!" Chest compressions are started again. "We got a pulse!" Sunny's heart starts beating. She is still unconscious. The medical team intubates her and hooks her up to the breathing machine. She is stabilized. Critical, but stabilized. "Don't you quit on me Sunny. You keep fighting. I'm Dr. Raji. I want to see your pretty eyes tomorrow. You rest up tonight. Let's get her to the trauma unit STAT. Call them now and tell them we're coming." The emergency medical staff transfer Sunny to the trauma unit where she will be in the toughest fight of her life.

Ahmaad's phone is ringing nonstop. He called Sunny's parents and told them as much as he could and urged them to get to the hospital to be by Sunny's side. He couldn't see Sunny like this. He couldn't see her die. He was blinded by rage and vengeance. "This coward ass bitch. I'm going to kill this bitch. He took my soul. My fucking soul. I'm going to kill this faggot bitch!" Ahmaad is shaking with rage while driving 90 miles per hour down telegraph road to get to Inkster. He is covered in Sunny's blood.

It's on his hands, his face and his white dress shirt which now looks like a red tie dye shirt. He doesn't even notice. He can't see anything except vengeance. He wants to kill Ezra so bad he has a full erection. He gets to Rosewood St. and sits at the corner which is about 6 houses away from Ezra's grandmothers. He sits and scopes out the house. Ezra's grandmothers house sits in front of a wooded area which is behind a golf course. Ahmaad parks his car and walks thru the woods to creep up Ezra's back yard. It's dark with the exception of the light in the back of the house.

Ahmaad sees a cement block on the patio. He grabs his 9mm Sig Sauer with his right hand, cocks the chamber and aims for the patio window. He swings the cement block in his left hand back and forth; trying to gain momentum. On the third swing he lets the block fly into the patio glass door. Glass crashes everywhere. Ahmaad jumps through the broken sliding glass patio door and looks around and aims; ready to shoot anything crossing his path. "What in heavens sake! Hello? Help! Hello? Ezra? What is that noise?! Help somebody!" Ezra's grandmother is in her room in the back of the house, frantic; unaware of what's going on. Ahmaad walks towards her room with his pistol aimed and finger on the trigger ready to squeeze it. "Ahhhh help me! Somebody help me! Oh Jesus lord don't kill me! Jesus please help me!" Ezra's grandmother is terrified. Screaming at the top of her lungs.

"Shut up! Shut the fuck up lady!" Ahmaad yells at Ezra's 80-year-old grandmother as she sits in her reclining chair unable to move in her floral house coat and turban on her head. "I'm not going to hurt you. I want Ezra. You need to call him and tell him to come home. I need to see him now." Ahmaad demands. "What the hell you want with my grandson? You come breaking in here like this pointing that thing at me! What he done done? Just get my pocket book and I'll give you what he owes, but leave my grandbaby alone. Turn him loose. Now hand me my pocket book."

Grandma is pleading with Ahmaad. Ezra starts to calm down and realize the magnitude of the situation. He lowers his weapon and he starts to soften up. "I don't want your money ma'am. I'm sorry about your window. Just tell Ezra I'm looking for him. I'm sorry for this." Ahmaad walks backwards out of the room. Grandma is in her chair clutching her chest looking confused as Ahmaad walks out of her room and down the hall.

Ahmaad looks at what used to be grandma's sliding glass door and shook his head. He felt remorseful. *click click* The lock at the front door turns. Ahmaad grabs his 9mm and aims at the door like an assassin. Ezra walks thru the door with baby Caleb in his arms. "We home now lil man. You home where you belong." Ezra whispers to the baby. "Put the baby on the couch and don't you fucking move." Ahmaad sternly says to Ezra without raising his voice. He walks towards Ezra with his pistol aimed directly between his eyes. He eases closer and closer until the barrel of the gun is resting against his forehead. "You might as well kill me muthafucka. You pussy ass nigga." Ezra spits in Ahmaads face, never taking his eyes off him nor his hands off of his baby. Ahmaad reacts before he can think and takes the butt of the gun and smashes it against Ezra's forehead knocking him out cold. Ahmaad grabbed the baby before Ezra hit the ground. "You ok lil man? Let daddy see you." Ahmaad looks over the baby to make sure he isn't harmed. Caleb is in one piece.

POW "Get the fuck out of my house!" Screamed Ezra's grandmother as she shoots at Ahmaad missing him and taking out the kitchen window with her tiny .22 pistol that she keeps in her bra the way Ezra taught her. "Don't make me shoot you old lady! Your grandson tried to kill Sunny! And before I leave this house he will pay what he owes and that's with his life. Now take your ass back in your room!" Ahmaad yells upsetting the baby as he begins to whimper. "Mm mm, Mm..." Ezra starts groaning as he is regaining consciousness lying in a puddle of his own blood from the 6-inch gash across his forehead. "Ezra? Baby is that you? My baby! Oh sweet Jesus Ezra! Get up baby!" Ezra grandmother shuffles her feet as fast as she could to get to Ezra.

She didn't care about the gun Ahmaad had pointed at her, the baby or the news Ahmaad just shared about Sunny. She had to protect her grandson. Ahmaad knew he had to let it go. He didn't have it in him to hurt an 80-year old woman and she made it abundantly clear he would have to in order to get to Ezra. She cradles Ezra in her arms trying to wake him up. "I have an attempted murder suspect in custody at 27997 Rosewood St in Inkster. He shot my fiancé tonight and I apprehended him at this address. Please send units out immediately. I have my weapon drawn on him and I do have a license to carry. Thank you." Ahmaad ends the call with the 911 operator. Ahmaad walks over to Ezra and his grandmother with his step son cradled in his arms. Rage starts overpowering him. He knows he has to go before the police comes to avoid being arrested.

WAM Ahmaad kicks Ezra in the back of his head with so much force, his head propelled forward hitting his grandmother in the face knocking her unconscious and Ezra falls back into his state of unconsciousness with blood gushing from the front and back of his head. Ahmaad cradles baby Caleb even tighter and walks out of the front door towards his car. Ahmaad is driving down 94W to Ann Arbor to get to his Sunny. Baby Caleb is resting in his arms while he drives. Ahmaad is in autopilot. He can't feel anything he just knows he has to get to his Sunny. He arrives at the emergency entrance and he sees

Sunny's stepdad on the phone in the waiting area. "My God. Boy is you alright? Is that baby alright?" Sunny stepdad asks Ahmaad extremely concerned, but relieved at the sight of them. "Yes sir. We both alright. Sir where is my Sunny? Take us to her please." Ahmaad pleads with Sunny's stepdad. "Come on son." Ahmaad follows close behind holding baby Caleb tight against his chest. The walk seems like the longest walk he's ever had to take. The smell of cleaning agents and pharmaceuticals filled his lungs. Brown walls and bright lights and beeping machines overloads his sensory. The wind is knocked out of him when he sees Sunny. Lying on this ICU bed with tubes sticking out of her arms, chest, stomach, mouth, nose. Her face and body swollen.

She's almost unrecognizable. Sunny's mother is trying to dry her eyes and face with tissues that are saturated with her tears. "Son, let me have the baby and you sit down next to Sunny." Sunny's mom says with a very caring and concerned tone. Ahmaad is shaking. His autopilot has turned off. His adrenaline is depleted. He feels emotions raging through his body. He doesn't want to let baby Caleb go. Sunny's mom tries to take the baby from his arms but he holds on tighter.

"It's okay now son. It's okay. Let me have the baby son. You saved him. You saved my family son. Sunny will be ok. Let me have him." Ahmaad reluctantly lets baby Caleb go to his grandmother. He collapses into the chair and starts crying. Unable to stop. He grabs Sunny's hand and he weeps like a baby. "I got Caleb back baby. You can wake up now. Baby I just need to see your eyes. I need you Sunny.

Don't you leave me. Not right now. Not never. Sunny I need you." Sunny's mom tells Ahmaad not to worry about baby Caleb and she's taking him home so he can stay by Sunny's side. He agreed and thanked her. Ahmaad refused to go home until Sunny woke up. He was still wearing her blood. The ICU nurse gave him a pair of scrub pants, top and shower supplies so that Ahmaad could at least change into something clean.

Ahmaad went to the family restroom to shower and change. He closed the door and locked it so the sign would change to occupied. This is the first time he's looked into a mirror since he found Sunny drowning in her blood. Blood smears were painted across his cheeks and forehead. He looks down at his clothes and notices for the first time all the blood. So much blood. Ahmaad started to shake. His breathing became fast and labored. He tried to unbutton his shirt but his hands were shaking violently. He rips his $250 Armani shirt off out of frustration causing all of the buttons to pop off and land all over the bathroom floor. He turns the shower on all hot water. Ahmaad slides his shoes off and takes the rest of his clothes off. He gets inside of the shower and when the water touched his skin he completely lost it. He fell to the shower floor and cried his heart out. The magnitude of the events today hit him at once. He couldn't hold himself together another moment. He released everything he had. The water temperature started to drop. Ahmaad feels a sigh of relief; he washes the blood off him and puts on his scrubs.

Walking back towards the room, Ahmaad notices what seems to be two detectives walking about 20 paces ahead of him. He's worked around law officials long enough to spot them in a crowd. He doesn't know if he should turn around or go back to the room and hear what they have to say about what he did to Ezra at his grandmother's house. "Fuck it. This shit needs to be handled." Ahmaad says to himself aloud. He follows the detectives into Sunny's room. "You gentleman looking for me I suppose." Ahmaad states to the detectives with a cocky tone. "Ahmaad Johnson, we need to speak to you about some things that happened today." Says the white detective as his partner "the black one" looks at Ahmaad intently; never taking his eyes off of him.

Ahmaad walks back over to his uncomfortable reclining chair next to Sunny's bed, grabs her hand and sits down. "First things first. I'm not leaving my fiancé's side unless you force me to. If I'm not under arrest you two can ask whatever questions you like within the confines of this room." Ahmaad says sternly. Spoken like a true lawyer. The black detective clears his throat before speaking, "Look brutha. I know your circumstances are heavy right now but you can't throw bricks through windows and put someone in the ICU. You can't take the law into your hands Ahmaad. You're under arrest for breaking and entering and assault with intent to cause grave bodily harm. Please stand and put your hands behind your back." Ahmaad drops his head. He knows there's nothing he can do at this moment except follow the commands of law enforcement.

"Listen, I'm asking for mercy. Can you at least give me some time with my lady? I'm not a flight risk. Just give me an hour and you can take me in. Have some mercy, please." Ahmaad pleads. "One hour and we'll be back." The white officer retorts. Ahmaad bows his head in gratefulness. Ahmaad leans into Sunny's ear, "Baby, I have to go away for a few days. They charging me for whooping that hoe ass nigga ass. Baby open your eyes for me. Please bae I really need to see your eyes before I go. This is the only way I'll survive this bullshit Sun. Just let me know you're alright or at least you're gonna be." Ahmaad holds onto Sunny's hand as hard as he can without hurting her and he lays his head down and starts to pray silently. "Mmmm." Sunny moans sounding raspy and hoarse with tubes down her throat. Ahmaad almost fell out of his recliner.

He popped his head up so fast when he heard Sunny's angelic voice. "Baby! Sunny you're awake! Baby, oh my God baby! I love you baby! Thank you God! Thank you! Nurse! Nurse! She's awake! Get her some juice please or something!" Ahmaad sprints out of the room to get the doctors and nurses inside Sunny's room to assess her. They won't let Ahmaad back in until they've finished extubating her. Ahmaad sees the detectives walking down the hall. "Come on

God. Don't do me like this! You just granted my prayer now I have to leave her! Damn!"

"You ready Mr. Johnson?" Says the white detective. "Listen, she just opened her eyes. She just woke up y'all, please give me some time with her. I'm begging you both to please have some compassion. I just need 10 minutes with her; 10 minutes and you guys can do what you have to do." Ahmaad is pleading with the detectives.

They feel a great deal of sympathy for him, but they also have a job to do. "Alright look brutha. Tend to your wife. We will be back in the morning. At that point our hands are tied and we have to bring you in no questions asked. Don't make me regret this." Ahmaad thanks the black detective. Shaking his hand with tears welling in his eyes. The doctors are still inside Sunny's room. Ahmaad is pacing the hallway.

He is filled with so many emotions. “Ahmaad, you can come in now.” The nurse tells Ahmaad.

Sunny is sitting upright breathing on her own without any tubes down her throat. She has oxygen in her nose, and IV tubing running every which way. She's very pale and weak but she is awake. “Ahmaad.” Sunny says almost whispering. Ahmaad couldn't hold back his tears. They streamed down his face. He walks over to Sunny and plants kisses all over her face. “Baby, I'm so happy you're awake. I love you so fucking much baby. My Sunny. My sweet Sunny.”

Sunny is weak but happy to see Ahmaad. Her memory is foggy but she is coming around. “Where is my baby? Is he ok?” Sunny asks. “He is fine baby. He's with your mom. She offered to help out until we get you back on your feet. Baby listen. Tomorrow I have to go to jail.” Sunny interrupts Ahmaad with her raspy hoarse voice, “Jail? Did you kill him? Jail?” “No bae but I should have. I just roughed him up and so I have to turn myself in. It's protocol. I'll probably be out at the end of the day. But right now I want to focus on you. I was so worried about you Sun. I thought I lost you. I couldn't go on If I lost you Sunny. I want you to be my wife. I need you Sunny. I need Caleb. After we get you out of here we're going to plan the grandest wedding anyone's ever seen. I love you Sunny Johnson.” Ahmaad says to Sunny while sitting next to her, holding her hand and professing his undying love.

“I like the sound of that Ahmaad.” Sunny slurs as she drifts off to sleep. Ahmaad spent the entire night watching Sunny. The most she would stay awake for is 10 minutes. She's lost a lot of blood and her body needed time and rest to recover from the trauma. While Sunny rests, Ahmaad makes phone calls to every criminal defense lawyer and cop he's ever met. He tells them his situation and they tell him to sit tight until tomorrow.

Ahmaad didn't sleep a wink. His nerves wouldn't let him. Sunny's parents are knocking at the door with baby Caleb in tow. "Hey daddy's baby. Hey man!" Ahmaad says as he reaches for Caleb. "How is she? What are they saying Ahmaad?" Sunny's mom asks. "She's in for a long haul but she's strong. Her memory is still foggy but she knows what happened to her." "Hi ma." Sunny chimes in. "Sunny oh my baby. It's so good to hear your voice! You look good girl! Your color is back and everything. You ready for your track shoes yet?" Sunny's mom jokes. "Is that my baby? Is that mamas baby?" Sunny says talking to Caleb. Caleb instantly starts cooing and smiling. Ahmaad gently places Caleb onto her chest. Sunny starts sobbing uncontrollably. "I thought I'd never see you again. Thank you God. Thank you God. Thank youuuu!" Sunny sobs while embracing her baby as tight as she can with her weak arms. Sunny and her family sit in her room and try to lift her spirits. No one wants to even utter Ezra's name.

All day family and friends have been in and out of Sunny's room except Tyra. Ahmaad hasn't heard from her since she called him to find out what was going on. And what's even more peculiar is the detectives never came back to the hospital and its now nightfall. Ahmaad decides to check his messages after Sunny went back down for a nap and everyone's gone for the day. "36 messages. Are you kidding me? Ugh." Ahmaad says to himself in an annoyed tone as he pushes the play option to listen to his messages. "Ahmaad this is detective Stern. We don't need you to come downtown after all. You're in the clear. You take care of yourself and your beautiful lady. If you have any questions, feel free to call the precinct." Ahmaad saves the message and hangs up the phone. He gets on his knees and thanks God for granting him his prayer...Mercy. "Baby, baby can you hear me? I don't have to go to jail. Everything is taken care of." Ahmaad whispers in Sunny's ear. Sunny awakens. "Thank you Jesus. Bae I need you to do me a favor." Sunny asks. "Yes baby, anything." Ahmaad answers.

"I need you to go home get in the shower; wash your balls and armpits really good and brush your teeth. And just chill. I'm alright here for a little while. And I need my phone so can you bring it back with you?" Ahmaad is smiling and chuckling while smelling his rank armpits. "I don't want to leave you mama." Sunny shakes her head no, "Un uh you gotta get yourself together before you put me back in a coma." They both laugh. This moment is something they both desperately needed. “Alright I’ll be back as soon as I can. Ok?” “ok husband. I like how that sounds.” Ahmaad kisses Sunny passionately on the lips. He stares into her eyes and he’s just in awe of her strength and beauty.

Ahmaad hasn’t been home since the incident. Sunny’s blood is all over the bedroom. Ahmaad gets all the cleaning supplies in his house and starts cleaning and bagging the linen and pillows up for the trash. The room smells of bleach and Fabuloso. It’s as if nothing ever happened. Ahmaad finally takes off his musky scrub pants and top and gets into the shower. He’s so uptight he has knots in his shoulders and back. He needs to release some tension. He palms the head of his dick and makes circles. Blood starts flowing to his member. His erection grows harder and longer. He caresses the shaft and tightens his grip. He grabs the Irish spring shower gel and squirts a dollop on his hand and starts to stroke all 9 inches. His hand glides like a gazelle over his man pole. He picks up speed as he feels his semen building up inside his sack. He hears himself saying Sunny's name over and over. "Sunny.... Sunny...My Sunny...Open your mouth baby." He's imagining Sunny is in the shower with him jerking him off. He explodes all over the shower door. It looks like he squirted creamy white shower gel on the shower glass.

He feels relieved, relaxed and ready to sleep. Ahmaad dries off and puts on his pjs. He calls Sunny and tell her he will be back in the morning and wishes her a goodnight. "Baby don't forget my phone and bring me a notebook and my good pens." Sunny requested. "I got you baby. I'll be up there bright and early. I love you mama." Ahmaad ends the call. He looks around for Sunny's phone and finds it under their bed. It's dead of course so he gets the charger and plugs it up so it will charge while he's sleeping. As soon as his head hits the pillow, Ahmaad is out like a light for the next 8 hours.

The chirping birds and bright morning sun wakes Ahmaad from his deep slumber that his body commanded from him. Before he gets out of the bed to brush his teeth or grab a bite to eat he calls Sunny. "Baby how did you sleep?" Ahmaad asks Sunny over the phone. "Not the best but I'm okay. I miss you bae and my phone. Can you bring Caleb up here? I need to see my baby." Sunny requests. "I got you baby. Mama said she was bringing him up today. And I'm going to brush my teeth and be up there with your phone and pens and notes. I got you woman and I love you. See you in a minute." Ahmaad ends the call. He turns on Sunny's phone and gets himself together for the day. Sunny's notifications are beeping nonstop. Ahmaad is in his bathroom brushing his teeth. He's thinking of letting Sunny check her messages but he wants to make sure Ezra didn't send her anything that could be upsetting. He spits out the toothpaste and saliva and washes the remnants off the corners of his mouth. Ahmaad walks into the bedroom and picks up Sunny's phone. She has over 100 text messages from various people. He sees Ezra's number immediately and he opens the thread. The date goes back to the night he shot Sunny. It's pictures of him and Veronica. "This hoe ass nigga. I can't believe this nigga. Fuck man, how am I going to explain this shit." Ahmaad says to himself as he sits in disbelief.

Ahmaad doesn't delete the messages because they're evidence. He knows he's going to have to answer for the pictures but he knows he has time because the focus is getting Sunny healthy and back home. Veronica has been texting Ahmaad incessantly since Sunny's attack. Ahmaads been so consumed with everything he didn't even think to respond to her or let her know what was going on until now. "Oh, so now you decide to call me a week later? I know you have a ready-made family but what the fuck am I Ahmaad?" Veronica yells through the receiver of the phone. "Look V I didn't call to hear all that shit. I been going thru it and I need to talk to you. Are you home?" Ahmaad asks in an annoyed tone. "Yeah I'm home but that don't mean I want to see you, asshole. Next time you want your dick sucked stay home and ask your step baby mama." CLICK. Veronica ends the call. "This bitch has me fucked up." Ahmaad gets his shoes on and drives over to Veronica's. The way Ahmaad treats Sunny versus other women he doesn't share a deep emotional connection with is night and day. He treats Sunny with the utmost respect and dignity. He never disrespects her or speaks to her abusively. But Veronica….is a completely different story. He treats her as if she's just a random dispensable jump off. He doesn't even know why he kept messing around with her because Sunny satisfied him in every aspect of their relationship, especially sexually. He thinks the fact that Sunny made it known she loved Ezra more than she loved him bothered him. He felt like he had to keep "possible's" in the background just in case she was with him out of some irrational decision she made off raging pregnancy hormones. He wasn't secure with their relationship because of Sunny's lack of transparency with her feelings.

Ahmaad lays on the buzzer to Veronica's apartment until she picks up. "What nigga?" Veronica says through the intercom. "Open the fucking door V."

There's a 5 second pause and she hits the buzzer to let Ahmaad in. He walks up the stairs to her apartment and opens the unlocked door. Veronica is in her kitchen stirring pancake batter in her silver mixing bowl with thong panties, a wife beater and no bra. Her nipples are protruding thru her beater.

Her long jet black hair is pinned up in a brown banana clip with a few curly strands falling from the clip down her neck. He white thong panties show off her round voluptuous ass. Her bald pussy lips are too fat to be covered by the thin material in the crotch of the thong panty. Her sex appeal is on 10. Ahmaad's kryptonite. "V we need to talk about the other night. You may be summoned to appear in court." Veronica drops the bowl of batter and folds her arms. "What the fuck Ahmaad? What you mean "I may be" summoned?" Veronica shouts. Ahmaad tells Veronica about the pictures Ezra sent and what he did to

Sunny. "Oh my God Ahmaad. This is so fucked up. I'm sorry I gave you shit. Is she going to be okay?" Veronica asked trying to sound concerned but secretly wanting Sunny not to be okay so she can have Ahmaad to herself. She was in love with the man. "Yeah she's pulling through. But I feel fucked up for messing around with you and Sunny's been nothing but good to me. And so have you V but I've never lied about who has my heart. So I just want you to know what's up. I just need you to fall back. I need to give Sunny my all. She deserves that much. And you deserve a nigga that's all yours you know." Ahmaad says with all the sincerity he can muster. Veronica is quiet. She is staring into Ahmaads eyes. She won't ever let him go. She will get her man. "You never could resist me Ahmaad." Veronica says as she grabs Ahmaads hands and places his left hand on her pussy and his right hand on her ass.

"Come on V don't do this. What did I just say man? Chill." Ahmaad says through gritted teeth and a bulging erection. "I heard you but I need you Ahmaad. Once more. I deserve that. I need closure." Veronica grabs the back of Ahmaads head and pulls him to her mouth. She nibbles on his bottom lip. Then his upper lip. She slides her wet, maple syrupy warm tongue inside his mouth.

He welcomes her inside. Ahmaad grabs the back of her head with a fist full of her hair breaking the banana clip into pieces. He stares at her and all he sees is lust and the greatest tension reliever he can have at this moment. She is giving him a sexy smirk while wincing from the pain she feels from him pulling her hair. "Fuck me goodbye, Ahmaad. Fuck me like you love me for the last time." Veronica says while looking up at Ahmaad while he still has her hair in his fist with her neck pulled back. "You so fucking bad V. You a nasty little Puerto Rican bitch. Grrrr." Ahmaad can't resist. He must conquer Veronica's pussy for the last time. He releases her hair and spins her around as she faces her kitchen sink. Ahmaad places his hand on the back of her neck and pushes down causing her to bend over. 'SMACK' He smacks Veronica on her ass leaving his big manly hand print. 'SMACK' He slaps the other ass cheek so they both would have matching hand prints. "Ahhh papi! ¡Por favor, Jorderme papi!" Veronica begs in Spanish. "You know that Spanish shit makes my dick brick hard bitch. Say it again." Ahmaad demands disrespectfully. "Joderme Papi!" Veronica begs again in her native tongue. Ahmaad grabs Veronicas neck with his hand and pulls her against him. He passionately nibbles and licks on her ear while she grinds her ass into his crotch. He turns her around and puts his hand on the top of her head and pushes down. Commanding her to kneel. “Unzip my pants.” Veronica can hardly wait. It’s as if she’s opening a present on Christmas morning. “Un uh slower bitch. You know how I like it.” Veronica loves being dominated and degraded. It turns every sense that she has on 100. She slowly unzips Ahmaads jeans. She then unbuttons them. She slides her hands inside of his boxers onto his ass cheeks and slowly slides his pants along with his boxers down to his ankles. He steps out of them while taking his shirt off over his head.

Ahmaad’s dick looks to be about 10 inches long. Every vein in his dick is bulging through the skin of his shaft. He is ready to fuck. Pure mindless fuck. “Swallow my dick V. You bet not choke on all this meat either with your rice n beans eating ass.” Veronica chuckles, “shut up nigga and give me my dick.” Ahmaad grabs Veronica by her neck and pulls her to her knees. He has completely transformed into his alter ego. Sunny has never seen this side of him. "Who's dick is this V?" Ahmaad asks while tightening his grip around Veronica's neck. "Mine" Veronica responds almost struggling because of the grip Ahmaad has around her neck. "Ahmaad puts both hands around her neck and starts to strangle her. "This is the last time I will ask before you pass out. Whose dick is this Veronica?" Gasping for air Veronica says, "Sunny's. It's Sunny."

Ahmaad loosens his grip as a single tear drops from the corner of Veronicas eye. Ahmaad spins Veronica around and bends her over her kitchen counter. He rips her thongs off of her and slides his steel inside her sloppy wet pussy. He starts to thrust harder and harder. "Harder got damnit. Harder!" Veronica screams. Ahmaad starts beast fucking her. His dick is moving like a speed bag against Veronica's pussy lips. "Ahhhhh fuck! Help me

Ahmaad wait! Oh my God help me!" Veronica screams out in pain and ecstasy. Ahmaad is focused on one thing only and that's getting his nut out. The only sounds he makes is his balls smacking against Veronicas wet burrito and his labored breathing. Ahmaad stops stroking and grabs Veronica by the arm and leads her to her bedroom. He pushes her down onto her bed and straddles her.

Ahmaad pushes Veronicas leg back towards her head so that her ankles are near her ears. He slides his dick back inside the portal to her soul. Ahmaad rest his ankles on the back of Veronica's thighs to ensure her legs remain pinned back. His ass is facing her face and his face is facing her pussy, sixty-nine position. "Lick your fingers bitch. Don't act like you don't know what to do!" Ahmaad yells as he is pounding Veronica's pussy. "Yes daddy yes!!!" Veronica screams as she licks her index and middle fingers. She takes her wet fingers and starts to rim Ahmaads asshole. "Yeah, that's it. You know what daddy like. You trying to get this nut early." Ahmaad moans. Veronica inserts her index finger into Ahmaads asshole. This turns her on and makes her pussy dripping wet. So wet Ahmaad's dick keeps slipping out with each thrust. "Maad I'm about to cum. I can't hold it!!" Veronica moans. "You better wait for me V. Put them fingers in my ass! Now bitch!" Ahmaad demands.

Veronica slips her index and middle finger inside Ahmaads asshole. She is matching his dick stroke inside her pussy with her fingers inside his ass. Ahmaads asshole starts getting wetter and wetter. His nut sack tightens up. She knows he's about to cum but she wants him to cum inside her and she knows just the trick. She feels the sensation like she has to pee. She knows she's about to squirt. "Maad you feel my pussy tightening? Baby I'm about to nut! Baby don't you fuck up my nut! You keep stroking. Call me Sunny, Ahmaad. Call me Sunny got damnit!" Veronica voice is two octaves lower as if she is possessed. Ahmaad can't hold on much longer. She knows his weakness. "Sunny...you want to be Sunny, bitch? Huh? Sunny! Sunny get this nut!" Ahmaad tries to pull out of Veronicas pussy but the sensation is too much to overpower. She squirts all over his dick and asshole while she is hitting his prostate with each stroke of her fingers. Ahmaad is powerless. Every drop of semen he has inside of his nut sack is emptied into Veronicas pussy walls. They both let out animalistic primal moans of lusts and sin.

Ahmaad is panting, trying to catch his breath with his dick nestled snuggly inside of Veronica's lustful cavern. "Why you make me nut inside you? Get off me V. Move!" Ahmaad demands while trying to calm his breathing. Ahmaad leaves Veronica in her kitchen with semen seeping from her pussy running down her legs. He goes to her bathroom to wash the evidence of their sex off of him. Veronica follows him. "So your done now? You think you're done with me because your little girlfriend is in the hospital?" Ahmaad doesn't respond as his sudsy nuts rest in her basin ready to be washed clean.

"You'll never be satisfied with her. You can't even tell her how to fuck you right. You afraid she's going to find out about your little ass play fetish? Huh fuck boy?" Veronica teases. In an instant Ahmaad grabs Veronica by the neck and slams her into the wall. "This is what you want huh? You want me to fuck you up? You think you can get inside me and fuck with my mental? I will snap your fucking neck. Stay in your place." Ahmaad releases Veronica neck from his grip. "You need to get the morning after pill today. Don't fuck around V." Veronica sighs and rolls her eyes. "Give me the money and I'll get it nigga." She says.

Ahmaad dries his nuts off with her pink hand towel hanging on the towel rack and throws it on the floor. He gets dressed and reaches into his wallet to get $40.00. "This should cover it. Now look V. I can't do this with you. You gotta chill. I'll call you when I can." Veronica just nods her head while standing completely nude next to the door waiting for him to leave. "I told you I just needed closure. I'm good on you. Good luck with your life." Ahmaad stares at Veronica in a bit of surprise by her reaction. He's relieved but his ego is a little bruised because she's not giving him drama. "Well alright. Take care of that today. Peace." He walks out the door on his way to the love of his life at the hospital.

2

Sunny's parents, brother and baby Caleb are at her bedside as Ahmaad walks into the room. They all greet Ahmaad as he reaches for baby Caleb and makes his way towards Sunny to kiss her with his cheating lips. "How you feeling mama? I got your things." Ahmaad says. "Where you been? It took you long enough" Sunny says with an attitude. Ahmaad wonders if she can smell Veronica on him. He starts feeling guilty. "I'm sorry baby. I was more drained than I thought. I won't ever keep you waiting that long again." Ahmaad plants kisses along Sunny's forehead while cradling baby Caleb to his chest. "Damn a bullet won't even stop your ass from being bossy. Give the man a break sis." Sunny's brother says trying to break the tension in the room. And it works. Everyone chuckles even Sunny. "Shut up fat boy. You always got something to say. As a matter of fact, I need you to get me a laptop so I can do my homework." Sunny requests. "I got you sis. Now let me get outta here before her requests start getting more expensive. Love you sis." Sunny's brother says while chuckling as he leans in to kiss her goodbye. "And don't forget I need the new Microsoft Windows. Ok love you bye!" Sunny says to her brother.

Family, friends, doctors and police detectives are in and out of Sunny's room for the next few days. The detectives updated Sunny on the pending court dates. Ezra has plead guilty to attempted murder and kidnapping. There's no need for Sunny to testify. His sentencing is in 6 weeks and Sunny is still numb. She hasn't allowed herself to think about everything that has happened to her and to her family, especially Ahmaad. Anytime Ahmaad brings up what happened Sunny changes the subject or just plainly says I'm not ready to talk yet. She has built an impenetrable wall.

"Looks like we're setting you free tomorrow Kiddo. Are you ready to break out of here?" Dr. Raji says to Sunny. "Hell yes doc! Sign those discharge papers STAT." Sunny says to the doctor. Dr. Raji laughs as he knows full well Sunny was ready to go home the day she was extubated. "You're a very strong woman Sunny. Your recovery is astonishing. I'm sorry we met under these circumstances but I'm happy I know such an amazing young woman. You make sure to go to all of your appointments. You still have some recovery to do with your right arm and shoulder so I don't want you to push too hard, ok?" "You got it Doc. Thank you for saving my life. I've always wondered what my guardian angel looked like.... who woulda thunk it...My angel is a middle aged Indian doctor. Hee hee hee!" Sunny and the doctor both chuckle. "You take care of yourself my dear. Godspeed." The doctor pats Sunny on her hand and walks out of her room.

"I can't wait to get home and sit on your face." Sunny tells Ahmaad while he sits in the corner watching her interaction with the doctor. Ahmaad stands and walks over to Sunny's bed. "Music to my ears mama. I've missed my Sunny dew." Ahmaad says while caressing Sunny's right cheek and chin. "This Sun has gallons of dew for you too. I hope you're thirsty." Sunny says while biting her bottom lip. Ahmaad's blood rushes to his crotch. His pants feel tighter and tighter as his erection grows and stiffens. Sunny sees his dick imprint grow through his jeans and she starts rubbing the tip of his man pole. "Girl don't get me riled up. You know we still have to take it easy and you know I can't resist you, Sun." Ahmaad pleads. "I know my limits. I need you to take me home and let me unleash everything inside of me onto your dick." Ahmaad looks Sunny in her eyes. He leans in and kisses her gently, softly yet full of passion. He pulls back to stare into her eyes again. He's looking for her but he can't find Sunny. Her eyes are dark and lifeless. Ahmaad realizes at this moment, Sunny is forever changed. "Let's get you home mama." Ahmaad says to Sunny.

Sunny is finally released and on her way home for the first time in 2 weeks after being shot. Ahmaad pulls into their driveway and Sunny starts shaking. Ahmaad puts the car in park and turns off the ignition. He grabs Sunny's hand and starts praying. "Dear God, please give Sunny the strength and courage she needs to overcome everything that has happened to her. Please help me to be a source of light and healing for her. Guide our steps Father. Please grant us mercy and courage. In Jesus name amen."

Ahmaad kisses Sunny's hand. "Take your time baby. We don't have to go inside today. We can stay in a hotel. Whatever we gotta do to get through baby I got you." Sunny takes her hand away from his grasp. "So did you fuck her when you came home to get my phone?" Sunny says coldly. "Say what? Sunny what are you talking about?" Ahmaad says in a tone two octaves higher than his voice. Sunny clears her throat and starts wringing her hands. "Cut the shit. Let's get it all out before I walk back into this house. DID YOU FUCK HER WHEN YOU CAME HOME TO GET MY PHONE, AHMAAD?" Sunny says sternly. Ahmaad is nervous. His hands begin to sweat and his defenses start creeping through. "How could I fuck anyone with you laying up in a hospital with a bullet hole in you? Come on now Sun. Why would I do some shit like that? How could I? I know this is a process but you can't take shit out on me. I was about to throw my life away to avenge what he did to you. Don't play me." Ahmaad says in an annoyed tone. "You must take me for a fool Ahmaad. I know you saw what he sent. I know you know I know. So get everything out. All of it. Before I get out of this hoe ass car and walk into this piece of shit ass house." Sunny is yelling at this point as she took her seat belt off to turn her body to face him.

Silence filled the 2001 Expedition. Ahmaad kept shifting in his seat. He couldn't look Sunny in her eyes. He was wrestling with the truth and a lie. He didn't want to hurt Sunny but he knew if he lied about something this damaging she would never forgive him. "I'm sorry Sunny. I fucked up. I fucked her and I don't even know why Sun. As fucked up as that sounds I don't know why. You and I were at odds about that nigga and how you handled the situation and you not coming home and shit. It's no excuse but that's the excuse I used to make myself believe that it wouldn't be a big deal if I fucked ol girl while we were fighting. I hate myself for doing it. It will never happen again. You have my word." Ahmaad pleads. "Your word, huh? Tuh...what a joke." Sunny opens the door and eases out of the truck.

Ahmaad rushes to her side before she gets out to help her. "Sunny hold up you got to take it easy. Let me help you." Sunny smacks her lips and snatches away from Ahmaad's hold. Ahmaad unlocks the door and walks in first. He grabs Sunny's arm and helps her inside. She looks around the house. Trying to adjust and take everything in. She walks into the kitchen and looks inside of the fridge then the cabinets. "We need some groceries." She says. "I'll go to Farmer Jack's and get everything we need. Let's make a list. Come on baby sit down and let me take off your shoes." Ahmaad pleads yet again. Sunny ignores him.

She slowly walks down the hallway and looks into the bathroom. She turns the light switch on then off and continues to walk towards the bedrooms. She starts to tremble again. She feels like she's walking in quicksand. Her breathing becomes labored and fast. Sweat starts dripping from her forehead causing her bangs to stick. "Sunny? Baby you're shaking. I got you Sunny. Come here. I'm so sorry baby. I'm so fucking sorry."

Ahmaad holds Sunny and tries to console her as she completely loses her shit. Her legs give way and she collapses into Ahmaads arms. If he weren't holding on to her she would've hit the floor hard. She is sobbing uncontrollably. Ahmaad feels helpless, but he knows the only thing he can do is hold onto Sunny like he's holding on to her for dear life. "I got you Sunny. Let it out baby. I'm so sorry baby. It's going to be okay. I won't ever let that nigga hurt your or our son again." Ahmaad comforts Sunny.

Sunny starts to regain her composure. Ahmaad is wiping away her tears with his shirt. "I can't stay here. Take me to my mothers." Sunny says through her raspy voice. "Baby we can stay in a hotel. I don't want to be without you Sunny. I have to be near you as much as possible. Let's get a hotel until we figure things out. What do you say?" Sunny looks Ahmaad in his eyes and sees he's almost in a panic. But she feels like he's manipulating her. They both know if she is away from him it will give her time to think about Ahmaad's unfaithfulness and cause Sunny to pull away. "Sunny gets up off of the floor and walks into the living room and sit on the couch.

"My life is a joke. You're no different from this nigga. I call myself leaving my sons father so he would have a better life and be raised by someone I want him to look up to and come to find out y'all are the same muthafucka! Tuh! What a joke...This is why I won't ever be faithful to no nigga or bitch. Fuck love. Take me over my mothers. I'm over this shit." Sunny says boldly. Ahmaad's wheels are turning. "What do you mean you won't be faithful? So you saying you cheated, too? Sunny answer me." Sunny looks up at Ahmaad with as much hate she could muster, "I sure did. So what now? You're gonna shoot me too? Put me out of my misery already." Sunny says trying to fight back the tears.

Ahmaad stands in the middle of the living room in silence. Staring at Sunny. She didn't notice at the time but tears started falling from his eyes. She stared back at him until his stare became too intense. "And now I'm here. Stuck. Stuck with someone who doesn't give a fuck about me or my intentions. Because if you think I'm going to let you go that easily, you really got me fucked up. You're upset with me and I deserve it. So I'm going to take whatever bullshit you give me until you forgive me. But in the meantime, I need you to be honest with me and yourself. You're no better. I know you and Tyra fucked. The night Ezra fucked up your car. You didn't think I read those text messages in your phone? But did I bring any of that bullshit up, Sunny? Did I? Answer me got damnit!" Ahmaad shouts. "No! Fucking asshole! And so what if I let Tyra eat my pussy! I didn't let another nigga stick his dick in me. Who cares if I let a bitch eat me. It's not the same. You broke my fucking trust! It won't ever be the same between us and I will never trust you! I've been down this road before, I know how this shit plays out! So before I get too comfortable with you taking care of me and we both start cheating again, let me go!" Sunny yells.

"Neither one of us is making this decision right now. But I am making a decision for the both of us. We're going to a fucking hotel until further notice. I'll pack your bag so just chill." Ahmaad walks into the bedroom to pack their bags. Sunny puts her head into her hands and starts crying. She is taken aback that Ahmaad knew about she and Tyra. She started thinking maybe Ahmaad is right. I'm no different. So why not give each other a fresh start. "Alright I got everything. Let's go Sunny. I'm not taking no for an answer." Sunny gets up and goes to the car.

The car ride was silent. Ahmaad and Sunny were both in their feelings. They couple arrived at the Courtyard Marriott Hotel near the Detroit Metropolitan Airport. "Stay here while I get the room." Ahmaad says to Sunny who doesn't acknowledge him at all. She stares out of the window with her arms folded and a blank expression on her face. Ahmaad checks into the hotel, gets back into his car and drives around the back of the hotel to get to their room. Sunny struggles to get out of the car due to her injuries. "Sunny wait a minute! Stop acting stupid! Look, I understand you're upset with me but be mad all you want. Just let me help you. Ok? Damn! You're so fucking stubborn."

Ahmaad is clearly annoyed. "Fine. Let's go inside, I'm cold. Ahmaad held Sunny up while they walked to their room. Upon entering the room Sunny went straight to the bathroom and started to run her bath water. "Sunny, I got this. Let me do this for you. You don't even have to talk to me Sun. I'll sleep on that couch. Just let me take care of you. Ok?

Sunny?" Ahmaad pleads. "Okay." Sunny says begrudgingly.

Ahmaad runs Sunny's bathwater and undresses her. He helps her ease into the tub. "Call me when you're ready to get out." Ahmaad says as he kisses Sunny on her forehead. Sunny still doesn't respond. She sits back in the tub trying to adjust to the hot temperature of the water. Her bandages on her shoulder are soiled so she peels off the tape and the bloody gauze to let her bullet wound breath.

This is the first time she's been able to take a bath since being shot. The sound of the water dripping from the faucet into the tub calms her down. She scoops the water with her hands and pours it down her breast causing her nipples to become erect. She scoops the water and pours it down her breast again and again. Her hands start to caress her body. Causing her pussy to ripen with her juices. Her hands found their way to her pearl hidden behind her bulging lips. She massages her pussy lips. Running her fingers through her outgrown landing strip and slipping her middle finger inside to stimulate her clit. She makes circles around her clit using her index and middle fingers. Circles, circles, circles over and over until her clit protrudes through her fat pussy lips. Sunny's eyes are closed and she is giving into her sexual desires. She starts to moan as her clit grows bigger and harder.

Ahmaad is laying in the bed with his hands behind his head staring at the ceiling waiting on Sunny to call him when she's ready to get out but, he hears her moaning in the bathroom. Ahmaad walks over to the bathroom and puts his ear up to the door to listen. He cracks the door open in hopes of Sunny being too caught up into her own selfish desires to notice him spying on her and he sees Sunny's head thrown back. Her nipples at attention piercing the water and her right hand going to work on her clit. She's biting her bottom lip in hopes of muffling her moans, unaware that Ahmaad is watching her. The bathwater is splashing against her skin as her fingers glide faster and faster on her clit as she approaches climax. Ahmaad's dick is so hard it could break through steel. Completely turned on being a voyeur for his woman. He opens the bathroom door an inch more and it creaks. Sunny jumps and removes her hand from the confines of her second set of lips.

"So not only are you a cheater, you're adding peeping tom to your lists of character flaws?" Sunny says with as much attitude as she can muster. Ahmaad walks over to the bathtub and kneels down beside Sunny. He grabs her wash cloth and starts bathing Sunny without uttering a word. He washes and scrubs her body from her hair down to her toes.

Sunny is letting her guard down. He lets the water out of the tub and scoops Sunny up like a baby. He wraps her up with a fresh clean hotel towel and dries her off. He takes a second towel and makes a turban for her hair. No words are exchanged. He leads Sunny into the bedroom of the hotel room, sits her down on the bed, takes her towel off and starts to moisturize her skin with coconut oil. Sunny is enjoying being catered to.

"Why do you love me?" Sunny asks. Ahmaad doesn't stop rubbing the coconut oil into her legs and feet. He looks at Sunny with an intense stare. "I love you because the Universe ordered my steps into your life. I love you because my heart beats your name, my mind drowns in your eyes and between your thighs, my soul feels yours even when we're apart. I love you because I didn't nor do I now have a choice. I didn't need to love you, but I love you the same. My arms aren't filled unless you're in them and my thirst is not quenched unless you are the drink. My soul directed me to you and you are my mate. That's why I love you, Sunny." Sunny's eyes start welling up. Ahmaad caresses Sunny's face and leans into her. "I'm so fucking sorry baby. I'm so fucking sorry. I will spend the rest of my life making this up to you." Ahmaad says while planting kisses along Sunny's face and neck. Sunny gives into Ahmaad. She just wants everything to be over. She's tired of fighting. She wants to feel alive again. She wants to feel love. She wants to feel full from Ahmaad's cock inside her walls.

Ahmaads lays Sunny back on the bed. He opens her legs gently and trails kisses along her inner thighs. Causing her to arch her back the closer he kisses near her pussy. He kisses her pussy lips and trail kisses along the other thigh. "I've missed my pussy Sunny. I've missed her so much. I've been craving her for weeks. May I please say hello to MY pussy, Sunny? Is she still mine, Sunny?" Sunny looks at Ahmaad while biting her lower lip, looking seductively. "She's all yours Ahmaad. Take a peek inside and say hello." Sunny says coquettishly.

"Fuck a peek. I'm living inside her." Ahmaad puts his entire mouth over Sunny's pussy. He sucks on her clit, causing it to peek outside of its hood. He sucks and licks her clit until his goatee is coated with her juices. He moans with every flick of his tongue. He takes his fingers and opens Sunny's pussy lips as far as he can without hurting her. He stares inside her walls, watching her clear secretions ooze from her cunt like honey dripping from its comb. Ahmaad wants to lick every bit of her sweetness. He sticks his 6-inch tongue out and drives it inside her pussy. Lapping up every bit of her spicy sweet wetness.

Sunny closes her eyes tight and gets lost inside her body. Succumbing to the desires of her pussy. "Suck my clit Maad. Suck that muthafucka until I can't take it anymore." Sunny demands. Ahmaad rims the inside of Sunny's pussy walls, licking up the last bit of nectar. "Taste how sweet my pussy is, baby. I want you to see why you got me so fucked up." Sunny grabs the sides of Ahmaads face and pulls him to hers. She sucks all of her honey out of his goatee and chin. Moaning as if she's eating sweet apple pie. "I see now bae. I see why you love this pussy so much. Fuck me and show me just how much more you love it." Ahmaads 9-inch dick is so hard it's almost painful.

"You ready for this dick? Huh? Tell me you want this dick, Sunny" Ahmaad says while holding his rock hard dick in his hand at the entrance of Sunny's life force. Sunny grabs Ahmaads dick and rubs the head up and down her clit making her juicier. “Give me my muthafuckin dick nigga!” Ahmaad eases all 9 inches inside Sunny’s cunt. Causing her to scream out, “Got damn!” Sunny’s pussy was so tight and sloppy wet Ahmaad almost lost his load on the third stroke. “Sunny it’s too good, I’m about to cum bae. I can’t hold it bae.” Sunny pushes him off her and takes control. She pinches the head of his dick to stop his nut from escaping prematurely. “Ahhhh” Ahmaad whence. “You better not cum got damnit. You’ve been giving my dick away to that bitch with that wack ass pussy and now you don’t know how to act when you get that good good huh nigga?”

Sunny chokes Ahmaad with her left hand and gets on top of him. “Put that dick back inside this pussy got damnit.” Ahmaad can barely speak due to the tight grip Sunny has around his neck. But he does exactly what she commands. She sits down on his dick as it is nestled inside. She can't put any weight on her right arm due to her gunshot wound so she puts all of her weight onto her the hand that's around Ahmaads neck. She starts bouncing up and down on his dick. Coming down harder and harder with each thrust. Ahmaad face is turning red. He grabs her hand trying to loosen her grip. "Let my fucking hand go nigga! Let it go!" Sunny commands through gritted teeth. Ahmaad obeys.

Moans escape his throat through her death grip around his neck. He can't hold on much longer as he begins to lose consciousness. The feeling he has is extremely heightened. He feels hallucinogenic and euphoric. Like he just snorted a line of blow for the first time. He starts to quiver uncontrollably as he fills Sunny's pussy with his seeds. He blacks out. Sunny snatches her hand off his throat. "Baby? Baby?!" Sunny shakes Ahmaad while sitting on his dick as semen oozes out of her pussy down his ball sack. She shakes his head back and forth. Still unconscious.

"Oh shit. What did I do? Baby wake up!" Sunny eases off his dick, nursing her shoulder. "Ahmaad wake up baby!" Sunny is becoming frantic. She slaps him hard, out of fear. He starts to blink. Sunny kneels down and starts kissing him all over his face. "Baby, you're scaring me. Wake up. I love you baby, wake up for me." Sunny whispers in his ear. Ahmaad regains consciousness and he looks around the room as if to remind himself where he was. "I've never cum so hard in my life, Sun. What the fuck was that?" Ahmaad asks, dazed and confused. Sunny chuckles, and as she does her pussy muscles contract with Ahmaad's semi-hard erect dick living inside her walls. "Whoa whoa babe! Don't squeeze! Don't squeeze!" Sunny is tickled. She puts her hand on his chest and pushes herself off him as his dick slides out of her womb and falls onto his stomach leaving a wet sticky mess behind. Sunny lays down beside Ahmaad as they stare into each other's eyes with love and affection.

"Bae, did you choke me into unconsciousness?" Ahmaad asks quizzically. They both laugh out loud in unison. "Maad I swear I didn't mean to make you pass out. It was feeling so good I guess I lost control. I'm so sorry baby!" "Real talk…don't be sorry. Just do that shit again. I ain't never bust a nut like that in my life! I feel high as fuck. Come here girl." Ahmaad cradles Sunny in his arms as they drift off to sleep. Sunny wakes up in pain from her wound. She gets out of bed quietly as to not wake Ahmaad and she takes her Oxycodone. She sits on the couch waiting patiently for her narcs to kick in with relief.

Ahmaads phone is on the night stand illuminating from missed calls and text messages. Sunny's curiosity got the best of her. She takes his phone off the charger and goes into the bathroom quietly closing the door behind her. "His dumb ass doesn't even have his phone locked. Niggas are stupid." Sunny talks to herself. Ahmaad has 4 missed calls and 20 text messages from someone named V in his phone. "This is the Puerto Rican slut." Sunny says while reading text messages of her professing her love for Ahmaad and how his crippled girlfriend can't satisfy him like she can. And how he needs to stop living a lie and she closes by sending close up pix of her pierced clit and nipples. "This hoe got me fucked up." Sunny says to herself as she hits V's number on the phone screen calling her.

"I figured this pussy would make you call." Veronica says on the other end of the receiver. "Your pussy does look good. I can't front. So you got it bad, huh bitch?" Sunny says. "Hello? Who the fuck is this?" Veronica says. "You know exactly who this is. Say my name." Sunny demands. Silence falls between them*. Veronica hangs up the phone. Sunny calls back. "Don't hang up now, let's talk. You're ballsy enough to fuck my man and send him pussy pics surely you're ballsy enough to have a woman to woman conversation with me." Sunny says calmly.

"Look, you know we fucking! Ok, so now what? Your nigga ain't shit. Sorry you had to find out like this." Veronica says through her cracking voice due to nervousness. "Don't be disrespectful. You need to learn your place. He needs to teach you better. Better yet, I will show you the way. Why don't you meet with me for lunch in a couple weeks? Let's talk about this situation we have on our hands." Sunny proposes. “Um…are you serious right now?” Veronica asks. “Dead ass.” Sunny says. “Ok, lets meet up.” Veronica agrees. “My only requests is that you keep your mouth shut. Don’t tell Ahmaad shit. That’s the least you can do.” Sunny says. “Ok. Fine. I won’t say anything.” Veronica agrees. “I’ll be in touch.” Sunny ends the call. She’s not sure what exactly she wants to do with Veronica, but she wants to make them both pay.

She sends the pictures of Veronica’s pussy and titties to her phone for evidence and masturbation material. Her pussy started throbbing the moment she opened the pictures. Veronica was a bad bitch. She puts you in the mind of a Hispanic Rihanna. Sunny deletes all messages and calls from Veronica off Ahmaads phone. She creeps back out into the bedroom area of the hotel room and puts his phone back on the charger on top of the night stand and slides back in bed. He doesn't budge. She thinks to herself, "damn, I put it on his ass."

Sunny didn't sleep a wink. She was up all night thinking about everything that's happened to her. Being raped as a child, abandoned by her father, domestic violence, attempted murder. She shed a single tear that night and vowed to never cry again for herself. She felt like a different woman. She was turning into a true savage; allowing herself to be victimized by her circumstances. She gets out of the bed as the sun peeks through the hotel curtains.

She puts on a pot of coffee and turns on the news. "Good morning baby. How you feeling?" Ahmaad asks as he stretches and rubs the eye boogers from his eyes. "I'm cool just a bit tired. I didn't sleep much. Your ass slept like Caleb. I'm ready to go home and I want my baby home today." Ahmaad raises his eyebrows as if he's in shock or surprised at Sunny's request. "But baby don't you think we need a little more time? I mean you had a fucking panic attack just yesterday. We need to take things slow and Caleb is fine with your mom. We can go over there and stay all day. Put him to sleep and come back to the room." Ahmaad suggest. "Ahmaad, don't coddle me. I said I want my baby and I'm ready to go home. I know what I need. Don't try and psychoanalyze me. I'm not trying to be a bitch but nobody knows what I need better than me so let's go." Sunny demands. "Aight, Sunny. Alright." Ahmaad submits. On the car ride to Sunny's parents house, her mind raced a million miles per second. She felt anxious. The closer they got the more doubt crept in. She wasn't ready. "Just take me home. I'm not ready to get Caleb Ahmaad." Ahmaad looks over at Sunny with concern. Tears stream down her cheeks. "Ok baby. Let's get you home." Ahmaad did a U-turn to go back home. He grabbed Sunny's hand, held on tight and kissed the back of her hand over and over. "I love you so much baby. You're so fucking strong. We will get thru this. I promise if it's the last thing I do, we will get you through this." Sunny looked out the windshield with a cold blank stare and tear stained cheeks. She felt numb, cold. She didn't even realize she was crying.

3

It was if her body had to release all the emotions she was feeling but her mind was absent from her body. The two didn't connect. Sunny turned and looked at Ahmaad. He had tears in his eyes; He felt helpless. He's a problem solver. Mr. troubleshooter. Ahmaad has a solution for everything, but he couldn't figure out how to fix his woman. Hell, how could he when he hasn't figured out how to deal with his own trauma from coming home from work seeing his future wife shot, bleeding to death inside their home. He loves Sunny more than himself and the last thing he can think about is getting counseling for PTSD. His focus is getting Sunny back to the person she used to be. Sunny tugs at Ahmaads belt buckle. Unbuckling it. Ahmaad looks down at his pants, then the road, his pants, the road and finally Sunny. "Baby whaa, what you doing? It's broad daylight!" Ahmaad asks in a higher than usual tone. He's taken aback. "I love you too, Ahmaad." Is all Sunny says before reaching inside Ahmaads unzipped pants and pulling his dick out through the slit in his boxers. Sunny turns to her left side, being careful not to move awkwardly because of her wound and she deep throats Ahmaad's dick in one swallow. He swerves in and out of the middle lane on Telegraph Rd. Sunny pulls his dick out of her throat just to say, "you better drive this muthafucka straight. You know Telegraph hot." She gobbles his dick up, again, with one smooth head stroke immediately after she stopped talking. It's as if Ahmaads dick inside Sunny's mouth was the period of her last sentence. She's never been able to deep throat his big 9-inch cock until today. She bobs up and down in swift short motions. Keeping the head of his dick down her throat and her head just below the top of the steering wheel. She keeps swallowing to ensure his dick goes as far down as it can go. His leg starts shaking. They're approaching a red light. "Baby I'm about to nut and people can see us! Baby! Wait a minute! wait, wait, waaaaa! Ahhh! Unh! Ung! Ahhhh!" Ahmaad groans and moans through gritted teeth while clenching onto the steering wheel for dear life as his seeds swim down Sunny's esophagus. Slowly, she moves her head up, releasing his cock from her throats death grip. She politely puts his dick back inside his boxers and zips his pants while licking the corners of her mouth. Sunny was drunk off power and lust. She felt alive. Empowered. When she has sex she completely loses herself. Her mind escapes to the land of Euphoria. She doesn't think about her childhood, Ezra, almost dying, her son… All she can think about is reaching the pinnacle of pleasure; the giver and receiver of it. The couple arrives home.

Sunny's entire demeaner has changed. Something inside her changed. After being hurt yet again by someone she loved and trusted, she turned off every emotion she had for people; including herself. "Baby are you sure about coming back home? You don't have to push this; you know?" Ahmaad asks. Sunny looks at Ahmaad, strokes his right cheek, leans in and kisses him on the lips and opens the car door without saying a word.

They walk inside and Sunny takes a deep breath and buries every emotion tied to her trauma. She walks into their bedroom and lies down. "I need a nap baby. Can you do me a favor and get us some chronic? I feel like smoking. A lil Hennessey would be nice too." Sunny tells Ahmaad. "I got you bae. Rest up. It'll be here when you wake up." Ahmaad kisses Sunny on the forehead and heads out the door. Sunny hears the door close and she walks to the front of the house to peek out of the front window to make sure Ahmaad pulled off. Sunny gets her phone and calls Tyra. Tyra answers the phone but doesn't speak. "Hello? Hello? Tyra??" Sunny yells into the receiver. "Sunny is that you?" Tyra replies. "Yes bitch it's me! What the fuck, T? You didn't come to see me you didn't call you didn't text? How could you not be there for me? You're a real fucked up selfish bitch! So I'm making my rounds and cutting everybody the fuck off and you were number one bitch!" Sunny yells. "Sunny, are you fucking kidding me? So you have no idea what your man did to me? Did he tell you?" Sunny was about to hang up on her best friend. Her only friend. "What the fuck are you talking about Tyra?" Sunny asks sounding confused. "Wow. He didn't tell you. Your psychotic ass boyfriend went through your phone after Ezra shot you. I guess he saw our messages and pictures. He came over my apartment and threatened my life. He said if I didn't stay away from you he would kill me. He pulled a fucking gun to my head, Sunny! He's crazy and you need to leave before he be the next nigga to shoot your ass!" Tyra is crying into the phone. Sunny is in shock. She realizes she doesn't have a clue who Ahmaad is. "Tyra, why didn't you call the police?" "Because all the shit that was going on Sunny! I didn't know what the fuck to do! I knew the nigga saved you and Caleb and I didn't want to get involved. He fucking scared me Sunny! I never seen it until that day but his eyes went dark. His facial expressions changed. He morphed into a fucking demon! Please don't tell him Sunny. You have to get away from him though. He is fucking insane." Tyra pleads to her friend. "T I'm fucked up. I'm sorry he did that to you but I'm fucked up right now. I'm going to figure this shit out though. Don't worry I'm going to get his ass together. I'll talk to you later T." "Sunny wait! I fucking miss you! I need to see you. When can I see you Sun?" "Sooner than you think T. I'll call you." Sunny ends the call.

So many emotions are flooding Sunny's mental. She's pacing the floor. "I mean got damn! Is this what my life has come to? Is this what you put me on this earth for, God? Huh? To suffer? To be used and abused by every man in my life? All I ever asked you for was to send me someone to love me. That's it! And this is what you do? Well fuck you!! Fuck you muthafucka!" Sunny is yelling at God. Pacing the living room and flipping the bird to the heavens. She goes into the bathroom and tries to gather herself. She holds onto the sides of the bathroom sink and stares into the mirror. She looks into her light brown almond shaped sad eyes. Her tear stained cheeks. The sling hanging around her neck that's supposed to support her arm and shoulder while her wound heals from the bullet given to her from her first love. The man she thought she would spend the rest of her life with.

"I guess you just don't deserve love. I guess it just isn't meant for you Sunny. Fuck love. Fuck these niggas. Fuck it all! Ahhhhh!!" Sunny screams to the top her long and lunges her head into the mirror, shattering it into dozens of pieces unto the floor and sink. Blood starts to trickle down her forehead. She wipes the blood and starts laughing uncontrollably. "I can't believe that actually made me feel better hahaha! Even I get off on hurting myself. Well fuck me." Sunny says to herself. She cleans up the mess she's made of the mirror and the 1-inch gash on her forehead before Ahmaad returns home. Now, she can finally rest.

A month has passed since Sunny's been home. She feels like she's made a full recovery. She has some soreness still in her chest but overall she's back to normal. Caleb is back home with Sunny and Ahmaad but her mother helps her out with caring for baby Caleb. Everything seems to be back to normal. Just the way she wanted it to seem. "Baby come on we're going to be late! The sentencing starts in 30 minutes' bae." Ahmaad yells down the hall as Sunny takes her time making sure every hair is intact and every curve is popping. She has on a very form fitting peach pencil skirt with a white blouse that has a plunging neck-line showing off every bit of cleavage she can get away with showing in a court room. Gold accessories and a pair of 6 inch beige Louboutins, Ahmaad gifted her: Probably for feeling guilty for fucking his Puerto side of ass she thought to herself immediately after opening the box. Her hair was pinned up into a messy bun with a couple of big wavy curls hanging at the nap of her neck. She looks into the full length standing mirror in their bedroom. She turns to the side to check her ass out. "Damn bitch. You're ready." She says to herself.

She grabs her camel haired mid-length pea coat and walks out the room. "Come on bae I'm ready." Sunny says to Ahmaad. "Damn. You look.... Great." Ahmaad says with his mouth hanging open. "Thanks baby." Sunny leans in to kiss him on the cheek. She can't mess up her makeup until after the sentencing is over. They arrived at the 17th district court in Redford just in time. As they walked in the deputies escorted Ezra into the courtroom from the holding are in the back. Sunny and Ezra lock eyes. She felt a cold chill run down her spine. Her cheeks turned rosy. Ahmaad was holding her hand tight. "I got you baby." He whispers into her ear. Ezra's upper lip twitches as his face turns into a grimace. They sit in the front directly across from Ezra's grandmother, mother and siblings. Sunny looks at every single one of them and no one would look at her. Not even the grandmother. "All rise, court is now in session.

The honorable judge Mahoney is presiding. You may be seated." The bailiff concludes. "Docket number 98765-B the people versus Ezra Carmichael. Mr. Carmichael, you plead guilty to 1ST degree attempted murder, kidnapping and child endangerment?" Judge Mahoney asks. "Yes your honor." Ezra states. "Before I sentence Mr. Carmichael, the courts would like to give the victim an opportunity to address the offender." Sunny clears her throat. Ahmaad stands up and helps her to her feet. "You're the strongest woman I know Sunny." Ahmaad whispers in her ear. Sunny squeezes his hand and walks to the podium. She adjusts the microphone so she can face Ezra. "I'm still here. You lose. You lost me, your son your freedom and hopefully your life after the judge reads his sentence. Rot in hell you piece of shit." The court gasps.

Sunny walks back to her seat with her head held high and with the grace of a swan. Ezra's family still refuses to make eye contact with Sunny. She made sure to look at each and every one of them as she walks down the aisle. "Well Mr. Carmichael. When I first read over your case, I was in disbelief. I asked myself, what on earth would drive a man to shoot the mother of his 1st born son. A woman whom he had great affection for since grade school. I couldn't think of not one reason. Your actions are despicable.

Thank God your son still has his mother, because he's definitely lost his father. The state sentence's you, Ezra Carmichael to life in prison with the possibility of parole after 256 months' time served. The court-room gasped. "No! Not my grandson! Turn him loose! That nigga right there tried to kill me! He the one need to be in jail! Turn my grandson loose yam hear me!" Ezra's grandmother shouts in the court-room.

Ezra turns to look at his family and he sheds a tear as the sheriff's usher him back to the holding cell. "I got you baby, let's go. Let's get you out of here Sunny." Ahmaad urges Sunny. More deputies rush to Ezra's family to escort them out of the court house before pandemonium broke out. Ahmaad and Sunny make it to the car unscathed and unbothered by Ezra's family. "That old bitch is crazy. How dare she! I should've beat her old ass while I had the chance!"

Ahmaad rants. Sunny is stoic. Staring out the window in silence. She turns and looks at Ahmaad. She finally sees a glimpse of his dark side he's yet to show her but unleashed on Tyra, Ezra and his grandmother. She turns her head sideways as if she's looking at stranger. But she keeps her composure. "Let's go Maad. Take me home." Sunny turned up the radio on the ride home to deter Ahmaad from talking to her.

She needed the time to push her emotions down even further. They arrive home and Sunny walks straight to the kitchen to pour a glass of Hennessey. She downs a double shot in one gulp. She pours another and decides to sip because Ahmaad is watching her like a hawk. "Let me see your phone, Ahmaad." Ahmaad looks at Sunny quizzically, raising his right eyebrow. "For what?" He asks. Sunny smirks. She wants to cut into him but she knows it will ruin her ultimate payback. "You got something to hide? Hehehe. Just cut your phone off. I don't want any interruptions." Sunny says while changing her mind about sipping slow and downing another double shot without breaking her stare from Ahmaads eyes. "Baby you know I don't have anything to hide I was just curious. But here you go. Turn that muthafucka off." Ahmaad hands her the phone.

She cuts it off and tosses it on the kitchen table. The two double shots kicked in quick. Her legs and pussy feel warm and tingly. She takes the bobby pins out of her bun and let her hair fall down her back. Ahmaad is enjoying the show. He can't help but to think something isn't right emotionally with Sunny. She shows little to no emotion and she doesn't want to talk about the sentencing. But he talks himself out of bringing up his concerns out of his own selfish desires and his weakness for Sunny's sweet spot.

Sunny walks over to the kitchen sink. She hikes her peach pencil skirt up exposing her bare ass. She bends over the sink and spreads her legs wide to expose her pussy lips. Her 6 inch Louboutin's make her legs look 7 feet long. She looks over her shoulder seductively and says "Come get this pussy, Ahmaad." Ahmaad is biting his lower lip. He strolls over to Sunny and smacks her bare ass leaving his hand print. Sunny winches. "Harder." She says.

Ahmaad takes his belt off and gives her two lashes on the same ass cheek. Leaving welt marks across his hand print. "I got something harder for you, got damnit." Ahmaad says while dropping his trousers. He spits on his hand and rubs the spit on the head of his cock. He places his belt around his neck and opens Sunny's ass cheek with his left hand and guides his dick in with his right. They moan harmoniously. Ahmaad slow strokes Sunny. His dick is covered in her creamy nectar. He leans over and nibbles her ear. Sunny turns just enough to look him in his eye and grab his belt. She tightens it around his neck as if it were a noose. “I thought you said you had something harder, Ahmaad? Fuck me harder!” Sunny demands while tightening the belt around Ahmaads neck. He starts pounding Sunny’s walls ferociously. Sweat starts beading on his forehead and down his back.

Sunny is staring into his eyes. Searching for Ahmaad’s secrets. His skeletons. She lets the belt go and smacks him across the face hard. The smack echoes throughout the kitchen. “What the fuck?!” Ahmaad stops thrusting. He rubs his jaw. Sunny doesn’t break her stare. She smacks him again. “I said harder didn’t I? Fuck me like I need to be fucked.!” Ahmaad picks up Sunny like a toddler and tosses her on top of the kitchen table. He turns her around and rips her blouse off; Then, tears her bra off breaking all three hooks. He stuffs his mouth with her breast and sucks and bites until she screams. "Shut the fuck up and turn around." Ahmaad spins her around and spreads her hands across the kitchen table as if she's being nailed to the cross. He opens her ass cheeks and spits on her asshole.

He rubs the head of his dick around Sunny's puckered virgin asshole and he puts the head of his dick inside Sunny's ass. Sunny whimpers. He slowly eases his dick inch by inch until Sunny started groaning in pain and pleasure. He picks up his speed, thrusting harder and harder. Sunny lets out deep belly moans. Moans he's never heard before. Her eyes are rolling in the back of her head. Tears are running down her cheeks. Juices from her pussy ooze down her lips and start to pool on the kitchen table. She's never felt this kind of pleasure. She's in pure ecstasy. She grips the sides of the kitchen table as the gates of her desires burst open and squirts all over Ahmaads balls. He can't stop. He pounds even harder, faster. He closes his eyes as he grabs a fist full of Sunny's hair. He yanks her head close to his chest and explodes inside her ass. He lets out the most primal moan a man can utter. When his dick released the last drop of cum Sunny pulled his cock out and stood up.

They're both out of breath staring at each other. Sunny sees his darkness. For the second time today, she finally sees the real Ahmaad. She goes into the bathroom and cuts on the shower. Ahmaad is on her heels. He walks into the bathroom and looks in the mirror. His right cheek is red and swollen from Sunny slapping him. "Damn Sun. What was that all about? You slapped the shit out me." Sunny looks at his face and burst out laughing. "Aww baby I'm sorry. I got caught up I guess. I apologize. You forgive me?" Sunny asks him coyly. "Mmmhmm" Ahmaad says. Sunny kisses Ahmaad on his bruised cherry red cheek imprinted with her hand and she gets into the shower. Ahmaad gives her privacy and leaves the bathroom. Sunny peeks her head out of the Shower curtain to make sure he's gone. She sighs. She grabs her loofah and loads it up with Oil of Olay shower gel.

Starting with her face she scrubs her body head to toe. She still doesn't feel clean so she washes the dirt and old soap off the loofah and loads more soap on. She scrubs her body. And scrubs. And scrubs. She can't seem to get clean. The skin between her thighs are turning red and burning from her vigorously scrubbing. Sunny collapses to the bottom of the tub and silently cries. She puts her hand over her mouth, balls up into the fetal position and cries as the shower beats down on her body. The door opens. "Sunny you aight?" Ahmaad asks. "Yeah, Maad give me a minute!" Sunny shouts. Ahmaad closes the door. Sunny stands up and lets the water wash away her tears. She is collecting herself and turning back into her alter ego. Sunny dries herself off and goes into their bedroom to put on lotion. Ahmaad is laying in the bed watching sports center. "Sorry baby I didn't mean to yell."

Ahmaad stands up, walks over to Sunny and grabs the sides of her face. "You sure you ok? You know you can talk to me. About anything Sunny. Even about Ezra. I can handle it." Sunny tilts her head to the side and says, "I know baby." Ahmaad grabs the lotion and moisturizes Sunny's skin from her forehead to her toes. He even puts her deodorant on for her. "Thank you baby. Hey I'm gonna go spend some time with Caleb and run some errands ok?"

"You want me to come with you?" Ahmaad asks.

"Nah it's cool. I'll be back shortly." Sunny gets dressed and heads out. She sits in the driveway and calls Veronica. She answers on the 4th ring.

"Veronica, it's Sunny. Can you meet with me today?"

"I didn't think you would call. Um yeah. I guess. I'm free now. Where do you want to meet?" without skipping a beat Sunny says, "Your place. I'll be there in 30 minutes." Sunny ends the call without giving Veronica a chance to respond. Sunny did some digging and found out where Veronica lived after the first time they spoke.

4

Buzz.... Buzz Sunny pushes the button for Veronica's apartment. "Quien es?" Sunny rolls her eyes and mumbles "this bitch so extra. It's Sunny, Veronica." 7 second pause goes by and Veronica buzzes her in. Sunny is wearing ripped jeans, thigh high black leather boots and a white button up form fitting blouse with the first 4 buttons undone, exposing her red bra and bountiful cleavage. Sunny walks up one flight of stairs. You can hear the heel of her thigh high boots pounding against the carpeted hallway. She gets to the door and knocks with her knuckle on her pointer finger. Veronica unlocks the door and opens it with the door chain still on.

She looks at Sunny and then looks down the hall to the left and right of Sunny. She closes the door, takes the chain off, opens the door and invite Sunny in by extended her arm. "Thank you for seeing me." Sunny says. "You're welcome. You can have a seat on my couch. So what exactly do you want Sunny?" Sunny looks around the apartment. She notices a club picture of Veronica and Ahmaad in her curio cabinet. Sunny smirks. "Cute picture." Veronica smirks back as she stands near her living room window with her arms folded under her breast. Veronica's wearing a bright purple sports bra with purple and black spandex exercise pants; white and purple air max on like she's ready for a fight or tae bo class. Sunny takes a seat on her leather couch. "Look V, this nigga played us both. My issue not with you, it's him. He deserves a dose of his own medicine." Veronica relaxes her arms and body.

She sits in her chair across from Sunny. "So what do you suggest?" Veronica asks. "I want you to get him over here. I want to see what he does and how far he goes. I want to ambush him." Sunny says stoically. Veronica laughs. "Soo you want to be hiding in the closet while he fucks me? Because when he comes over he's going to fuck me. He can't resist. I mean no disrespect to you." "That's exactly what I want. So what do you say?" Sunny says, expressionless. Veronica smirks, puts her hand over her mouth to hide her grin and walks over to the window. "So what if I don't want to leave him alone? What if I like the idea of you being with him and me dealing with him when I want? Did you think about that before you started plotting?" Sunny gets up and walks over to Veronica. She looks her dead in her eyes and sees Veronica is nervous and a coward.

Sunny moves Veronica's hair from her face.

She caresses the side of her face. She touches Veronica's shoulder gently and trails an imaginary line down her arm causing goosebumps to pop up. Sunny grabs Veronica's hand and says, "Veronica, we both know that's a lie. If you liked Ahmaad being with me, you wouldn't be so thirsty in his phone begging for his dick. Now you can continue to be a stupid hoe or you can regain some self-respect and boss up. You can have him after I'm through but just know once you get him my position becomes vacant and he will replace it with the next bitch." Veronica snatches her hand from Sunny. She was highly upset and turned on at the same time. She finally understood the power Sunny had over Ahmaad. She experienced it first-hand. Her sexual energy was intoxicating and addictive. Veronica had a small puddle in her thong panties. "You know what Sunny fuck you! You can kindly see yourself out of my damn house!" Veronica shouts.

Sunny looks at Veronica and sees how she's shifting between feet because her clit is swelling because she's turned on. Sunny thought to herself, "Got that ass." Sunny grabs the front of Veronica's sports bra and yanks it down exposing her 36D breast. Her nipples were swollen with lust and desire. Veronica tries to cover her titties with her hands, "What the fuck are you doing bitch!" Sunny grabs Veronica and stuffs a mouthful of Puerto Rican breast in her mouth. She starts tracing circles around Veronica's nipples with her tongue and then sucking. Circles and suck. Circles and suck. She nibbles the tip of her nipples as the stand at full erection. "Wha, what are you doing Sunny?" Veronica asks through labored breathing. "I have to taste you. Take your panties off. Now." Veronica looks at Sunny confused. But she does what she is told. "Slowly." Sunny requests. Veronica slowly peels her workout pants off her body; exposing her Purple thong panties with the entire crotch area painted with her pussy juice. Sunny grabbed a handful of her boyfriends side piece pussy and rubs her clit through the panties. She slips her index finger inside her pussy lips and draws circles around her slippery clit. Veronica is moaning and breathing hard. She wants Sunny. She wants Sunny bad. Sunny slides her finger out and a string of Veronica's wetness is holding on to Sunny's finger for dear life, begging her to come back inside. Sunny pushes Veronica down onto her leather couch. She kneels down and kisses the dripping wet crotch of Veronica's panties. Sunny takes her hands and rips Veronicas panties from her body. "Open your pussy for me. I want to see how beautiful she is." Veronica does exactly what she's told. She takes her fingers on both hands and spreads her lips open, exposing her Pearl.

Her pussy is so wet it had the nerve to make a smacking noise when she opened her lips. “Damn. I see why he’s willing to risk losing me. Your pussy is so fucking wet. I wonder if you’re as sweet as me.” Sunny says while looking up at Veronica into her eyes. “Only one way to find out.” Says Veronica. Sunny dives in mouth wide open devouring her clit. She makes the infinity symbol with her tongue on her clit over and over as her Clit swells and dances on her tongue. Sunny extends her tongue as far out as she could and slid as much as she could inside Veronica’s walls. She took her tongue out and rammed it back in. She did it again. And again. As if she’s trying to make her tongue nut. Veronica legs begin to stiffen and shake violently. Sunny feels the wetness of Veronica’s pussy trickle down her chin. She knew she was about to blow.

She went back to her clit and sucked like she was sucking Ahmaads dick. Veronica's clit got rock hard and started to pulsate violently. She sits up and screams at the top of her lungs while Sunny forces her face between her legs and continuing to suck her clit through her orgasm. Veronica tried to push Sunny's head but was unsuccessful. "Please please stop! I can't take it! Ok I'll do it! Fuuuuuuck! Sunnyyyyy!!" Sunny releases her clit and looks at her accomplishment. She stands up and wipes her face with her hand. Veronica is balled up shaking, trying to catch her breath. "I'm happy you see things clearly now." Sunny walks toward the back of her apartment trying to find the bathroom. She washes her face. Removing every essence of Ahmaads side bitch from her face. "So you think you can just leave like that?" Veronica says while walking up behind Sunny, cupping her breasts with her hands. Sunny smirks.

"Are you holding me hostage?" Sunny asks while looking at Veronica through the Vanity mirror in her bathroom. "I might be."

Veronica spins Sunny around and unfastens her button on her ripped jeans. She crouches down and unzips her thigh high boots and removes them one at a time. Veronica slides Sunny's jeans off. "Mmm no panties." Veronica says while her face is directly in front of Sunny's freshly shaven pussy. Sunny remains silent but never breaking eye contact. Sunny rest her ass on the basin and Veronica lift's Sunny's left leg and rest her foot on the toilet so she can just dig in without any road-blocks and that's exactly what she does. Veronica licks on Sunny's pussy like an ice cream cone. She's moaning more than Sunny is. "Your pussy is so got damn sweet. Fuck." Veronica says with a mouth full of Sunny's pussy, forgetting her table manners. Sunny tightens her grip on the bathroom sink. Her legs start to shake.

Veronica is going into overtime because she knows Sunny is about to climax. "Give me that nut. I heard you're a squirter too and I want it all in my mouth." Veronica says with a stuffed mouth. Sunny grabs a hand full of Veronica's hair and mashes her face in her pussy by pushing the back of her head. "Suck it harder. Harder got damnit!" Sunny yells. She's breathing hard, her stomach is twitching. "Open up your fucking mouth you dirty whore. Unnnn ahhhhhhh!" Sunny moans out in ecstasy as she pisses inside Veronica's mouth like a water hose. Veronica catches every drop and swallows it. "Mmmm yum." Veronica moans. Sunny smirks. She had every intention of letting Veronica make her cum, until, she felt she had to pee. She figured since Ahmaad just made her nut less than 2 hours ago it's no big deal. And the fact that he told her she's a squirter, made her want to desecrate Veronica's body; and that she did.

Sunny releases her grip on Veronica's hair. "Damn." Sunny says. Veronica gets up and tries to kiss Sunny. Sunny turns around and faces the mirror. She sees Veronica's cheeks turning red from embarrassment. Sunny grabs Veronica's hands and puts them on her hips. "Man we would have so much fun with you." Sunny says while looking in the mirror. Sunny turns on the water and grabs the shower gel. She squirts a dab in her hands and washes her kitty kat. "So you and him get down like that? I was under the impression you didn't" Veronica says while Sunny puts her jeans and boots on. "What do you mean you were under the impression?" Sunny asks. "Well it's just that he made it seem like you didn't get really nasty the way he likes it." Veronica says. "I take it you two have threesomes?"

Veronica shakes her head, "I mean no but he tells me what he likes. He likes when I talk dirty and I usually talk about me and you fucking him. And it gets him off." Sunny walks out of the bathroom to the living room. "What does he like? How do you fuck him?" Sunny asks. "He likes his ass played with. He ain't gay but he likes that freaky shit. He likes his ass fingered, ate the whole bit. And I guess he feels like you're just not that freaky ass bitch he needs." Veronica says. "Hmm. Interesting. So, then, Ms. Veronica." Sunny says while walking up on her. She's in Veronica's face and can smell her urine on her breath. "Are you down with what I suggested earlier or what?" Veronica was getting wet again. She didn't understand this sexual energy between them. But it overpowered her. "Yeah. I'll do it." Veronica says. "Great. I'll be in touch." Sunny grabs her purse and walks out without looking back. “That fucking bitch.” Veronica says while standing in her living room with cum sliding down her inner thigh and pooled on her leather couch.

Sunny calls Tyra. “You home? I wanna come over.” Sunny asks. “Yeah I’m home but Sun is that nigga following you? I don’t want him to know you’re over here. You’re going to have to do something with your car.” Tyra says in a stressed tone. “Ok T just come and get me from my mom’s. I’ll leave my car there but come now.” Sunny demands. “Ok I’m on my way.”

Tyra picks up Sunny and takes her to her apartment. They get inside and Tyra embraces Sunny. They haven’t seen each other since before Sunny was shot. “I missed you so much Sunny. So fucking much!” “I missed you too, T. I thought about you often. I’m sorry this nigga did that to you. I’m going to make him pay. Don't you worry." Sunny says while rubbing her friends back, soaking up the love she's giving her.

"Sunny fuck that just leave him. He is crazy! Do you hear what I'm saying? He pulled a gun out on me because I ate your pussy Sunny. Most niggas would want to join in or something but not him! Fucking Psychopath." Tyra scolds. "I hear you T but I gotta handle shit my way. You know that." Sunny takes a seat on the couch. "So where the drank at where the bud?" Sunny asks trying to lighten the mood. "I got some Hen in the freezer but I'm out of bud. Let me call my guy and see what's up." Tyra replies. Tyra gets on her cell and makes the transaction. "He on his way with the bud." Tyra pours Sunny a drink. Sunny slams it. "Dam Sun? Slow down bitch." Tyra says out of concern. "I'm grown. I need another." Sunny says while rolling her eyes. Tyra pours another one.

She knows not to contest her friend when she's like this. "So I heard he was sentenced today. How are you handling everything? I mean, for real Sun. How are you mentally?" "T, I'm fucked up, but what the fuck? What can I do bitch? I almost died. And I'm still here. So, I'mma just keep on living. I don't even see my baby T. My mama has him. I can't bring myself to take care of him because I'm fucked up T. I'm fucked up." Sunny starts shaking. Tyra rushes to her friend's side. "I know baby. I know. Let that shit out." Tyra holds onto her friend for dear life. Sunny let's out a gut wrenching scream and collapses into her friend's arms. They are sitting in the middle of the floor while Tyra rocks and embraces her friend. Tyra can't help but to cry with her... It's going to get better Sunny. You gotta get some help baby. You can't do this alone. I got you for whatever you need. Sun you gotta get out of this relationship and work on you and getting Caleb back." Sunny stops crying. She wipes her tears with the back of her hand. "Don't you think I know that T. Damn." Sunny scolds.

Tyra knows when to back off. Sunny gets up and turns on the radio. Tyra pours her another drink as someone knocks on the door. They both jumped. "Bitch who is that?" Sunny whispers. Tyra hunches her shoulders and walk towards the door. She looks out the peephole, "It's the weed man girl. We scary as fuck." Sunny burst out into a laughing fit. "What's up Dre." Tyra says as she welcomes the drug dealer inside. "hello ladies, what y'all into today?" Dre inquires as he checks out Sunny's figure while biting his lip as if Sunny's curves punched him in his dick. "Trying to get high. I hope you don't got no bullshit." Sunny says sarcastically. "Bullshit? Tuh! Tyra get your girl together. Ma, I am the crud God." Sunny swirls her drink in her cup with her hand while staring

Dre down. He's 5'10", 220 light brown mound of muscles. No facial hair what so ever with butter smooth skin. He has an old English "D" navy blue baseball hat pulled down low; a huge diamond encrusted Jesus piece draping his neck. Grey jeans and a clean bright white T shirt with grey Timberland boots to match; and, of course a pair of Cartier eyeglasses. Typical Detroit dope boy attire. "So pull that shit out Mr. Crud God. Let's see what you got." Sunny says in a sarcastic yet flirty tone.

Dre takes out a half eight and sits it on the kitchen counter. 'Fuck with me lil mama." Dre says to Sunny. Sunny inspects the weed. "It look aight." Sunny says dryly. "I tell you what…smoke this half on me. You like it, hit me up. But before I go you need to put my number in your phone. Trust me." Dre says to Sunny. Tyra looks like she's watching a ping pong match. Whenever Sunny was around, Tyra always seems to fade into the background because Sunny demands the attention of everyone in the room. Sunny gets her phone out and locks in Dre 's phone number. "Alright you ladies enjoy. Sunny? It's Sunny right?" Dre asks. "Yeah, it's Sunny." Sunny says seductively. "I'll be hearing from you tomorrow. Be smooth ladies." "Dre, say my name again." Sunny says to Dre as he's walking out the door. He smirks and chuckles and with every baritone octave he could muster he walks up on Sunny. He gets in her face as if he's about to kiss her and says, "Sunny. Sunny.... Mmmm, Sunny." And walks away leaving Sunny in a puddle of sunny juice. Sunny closes the door, "Damn Bitch!! Oh my god that nigga is sexy as fuck! I gotta hit that!" Sunny squeals. Tyra rolls her eyes. "There you go. Going after the wrong type of nigga again." Sunny rolls her eyes at Tyra and smacks her lips. "I didn't say I wanted to marry the nigga. I just want some dick. Back up off me." "Yeah ok. I'm just saying you don't want to get mixed up with his kind. He ain't nothing but a hoe." Tyra says.

Sunny gets in her friends face and looks into her eyes through her own squinty eyes. "You fucked him huh?" Sunny asks. "Move girl so I can break this weed down." Tyra says, obviously annoyed. "Bitch how was it?" Sunny asks. "It was cool. His dick aint big but he knows what he doing." Tyra says nonchalantly. "So you gonna be mad when I fuck him? Cuz I'm fucking him. Just letting you know." Sunny says while trying to suppress her laugh. "Do you bitch. You can have my sloppy seconds." Sunny pushes Tyra playfully, "Oh bitch fuck you." Tyra laughs.

The two friends laugh, smoke, drink and catch up on everything that's been going on. Neither one of them can get any higher and if they drink another sip of Hennessey they'll be taking turns on calling earl. "I'm floating. Fuck I feel good." Sunny says. "I know right. That nigga always has the best weed around." Sunny's phone is ringing. "Fuck, it's Ahmaad. Fuck ok let me get it together. Ahem…Hello? What's up baby?" Sunny says trying to sound as sober as possible through her slurred speech. "Are you drunk? Where are you? You've been gone all day and didn't check in." Ahmaad says with irritation in his tone. "I went out with some girls from school. They hit me up so I'm over Ashley's house and we're just smoking and drinking. And no I'm not drunk. I'm high as fuck but I'm not drunk Maad. Annnd I left my car at my mother's because I didn't want to drink and drive. See I'm being a good responsible girl" Sunny says through her lying teeth. "Did you spend time with Caleb?" Ahmaad asks.

Sunny knew better than to lie about this because

she's certain he spoke to her mother already. "No. I'm going to tomorrow. I just got caught up and let the time slip away." Sunny says with remorse. She starts getting emotional but she tries to hold back. "Sunny you gotta start getting Caleb. It's time for him to come home. You're better physically so it's no reason for your mother to have him. I know you going through something but don't forget you're a mother and soon to be wife. "Soon to be wife? Hmm, yeah I hear you. Just give me a break Ahmaad. I'll be home later. Not too late." "Yeah alright Sunny." Ahmaad hangs up. Sunny sits there and reflects on the conversation she just had. Ahmaad was right about everything. How could he be such a demented lying cheating abusive fuck and a great man at the same time? "I need a shot." Sunny says as she stumbles to the kitchen. "Bitch aint no more hen. We killed that fifth. And by the looks of it you're done-zo." Tyra says. "I'm so muthafucking, gotdamn fucking tired of everybody telling my grown ass what's enough for me or what's good for me or what I should be doing. I mean damn shut the fuck up!" Sunny yells at Tyra. Tyra didn't say a word she just let her friend take it out on her. Tyra decides to brew some coffee and start sobering Sunny up so Ahmaad wouldn't get any ideas and pop up over her house to make sure Sunny wasn't there. "You wanna smoke this last blunt or what bitch?" Tyra asks. "You know ittt!" Sunny says through giggles and burps. She plops herself on Tyra's couch while Tyra rolls the blunt and brews the coffee. Sunny takes off all of her clothes without Tyra noticing and she starts playing with her pussy. Tyra finished rolling the blunt and she looks up and sees her best friend naked on her couch fingering herself. She's instantly turned on. She missed Sunny's pussy. "So that's how you feeling?" Tyra asks while lighting the blunt and enjoying the show.

Sunny opened her eyes but didn't stop pleasuring herself. "Yes T. I gotta get this nut out. I been holding it in since this afternoon at that bitch house." Sunny replies. "Oh that prissy bitch. The bitch that tasted my yummy." Tyra says through taking drags of crud. "Come show your yummy why she shouldn't let anyone else kiss her, T." Sunny says erotically. Tyra pulls hard on the blunt and passes it to Sunny. I want you to finish that while I show MY yummy who's boss." Sunny squeals with delight. "Show her T. Show her got damnit." Sunny says anxiously. Tyra takes her time with Sunny. She kisses and licks on her nipples until Sunny started to cream. Sunny was on another planet. All of her senses were heightened. The weed intensified every touch every kiss every lick every suck. She pulls hard on the blunt and motions to Tyra. Pulling her to her lips and blowing the smoke into her mouth. Tyra inhales the cloud. She moves down her neck with her tongue. Driving Sunny wild. "Please T, put your mouth on it! I can't take it!" Sunny demands. "Shhh! Don't tell me what to do. I need to take my time and drink you in." Sunny groans. The anticipation is killing her but she lets Tyra have her way with her. Tyra gets up and goes into the kitchen to get some strawberries. She put some in a ceramic bowl and brings them back to the couch where Sunny Is naked, high and dripping wet. "Take a bite and give me that tail so I can put it out before you burn your beautiful nails." Sunny does what Tyra says. Once Sunny took a bite of the strawberry Tyra took the Strawberry and started making circles on Sunny's clit with it. Causing the strawberry to leave its juices all over her yummy. Tyra pops the strawberry in her mouth. "I've never tasted a strawberry this sweet, Sunny." Tyra says with seductive eyes. Tyra sucks the life out of Sunny's pussy.

Sunny opens her legs into a sideways split to ensure Tyra licks every inch of her yummy. Tyra starts humming on Sunny's pearl. "Oh my God T. The fuck? Are you fucking humming beauty by Dru Hill? Oh my goooooooooodddddd!" Sunny is going into convulsions. Tyra hasn't missed a beat. "I'm hoping I can make you mine. Mmm smack mmm. For another man steals your heart unnn mmmm slurp." Tyra croons with Sunny's clit in her mouth. Sunny body tenses up. She is completely tense and motionless. She's holding her breath. Soundless. Tyra knows to keep sucking her clit. Careful not to mess up her stride and keep the same sucking motion and intensity. She knows exactly when her yummy is about to release her sweet nectar. "T…Tyra. Do you feel my clit?

Baby do you fucking feel my clit Tyra? I'm about

to cum. Tyra...I'm about to muthafucking cum! Ohhhhh Shit!!!!" Tyra uses her mouth as a suction cup. Depriving herself of oxygen. Sunny clit hardens and shakes violently inside Tyra's warm mouth infused with strawberries and ganja. "Mmmmm mmmmm unggggg mmmmm!" Tyra moans in delight while refusing to remove her mouth from Sunny's love below until the quivers settle down and all the nectar is drunken. "Help me! Heeelllp me! Ok ok ok ok ok okaaaay!!" Sunny hollers out. Tyra pulls back off Sunny's clit. Sunny screams out in ecstasy while her pulsating clit slides against Tyra's wet warm tongue and succulent lips. Sunny turns to her side and balls her body into the fetal position. Her eyes shut tight, legs quivering, out of breath. Tyra watches intently as Sunny makes her way back down to earth. "Come here T. Come here." Sunny says.

Tyra slides her body on top of Sunny's and Sunny

starts kissing Tyra's face and lips over and over again. "I love you I love you I love you Tyra!" Sunny professes to her friend. "Muah Sunny you know I love you. "Tyra says while returning Sunny's kisses. "What the fuck am I going to do with you? Huh? Why can't you have a dick? Ugh! You're supposed to be my husband, bitch." Sunny asks. Tyra looks Sunny into her eyes and says, "Just don't ever stop loving me and don't ever leave me Sun." Tyra was madly in love with Sunny. She would do anything for her. Another casualty of Sunny's web. "I'll never stop T. Especially since nobody can eat this pussy like you do. You just keep me coming back for more hehehe. Girl let me get myself together and go back home."

5

Tyra didn't want Sunny to leave. She never does but something about this time made her feel like Sunny was using her. She felt used and discarded. She couldn't talk to Sunny about her feelings because Sunny would laugh it off and not take her serious. So she just held her tongue like she always does and waits for Sunny to get out of her car and deal with her emotions later. On the drive Tyra has flashbacks of the night Ahmaad ambushed her. She was coming home from work at midnight. Ahmaad was parked in her parking lot waiting for her. She thought he came by to tell her the latest on Sunny since no one returned her calls or text messages. She walks over to Ahmaads truck, "Hey Maad how's Sunny what's the latest?" Tyra asks. "She's going to be ok. Can we talk inside your apartment?" Ahmaad asks. "Sure. Come on up." Tyra leads Ahmaad to her apartment. She opens the door and tells him to have a seat. "I've been worried sick. I can't believe this shit." Tyra says while taking her coat off. Unaware that Ahmaad is directly behind her with his 9mm Sig Sauer in his right hand. Ahmaad grabs Tyra by her neck and puts the gun up to her right temple.

"So you've been fucking my bitch this whole time? You've been in my home, smiling in my face, eating my food, and eating my pussy? And you got the nerve to be calling me asking how MY bitch is? I should beat your muthafucking ass for the disrespect alone." Ahmaad says while talking directly into Tyras ear as she gasp for air and struggles to try to pry Ahmaad's hands off her neck. "Stop scratching me hoe and listen. Don't you ever contact Sunny again. You stay the fuck away from her. If you tell anyone about this, you will have hell to pay. And don't worry; I kept all those cute pussy eating pix you sluts shared on your phone. Stay the fuck out of our lives." Ahmaad releases his grip by pushing Tyra to the ground.

She crawled behind the couch and stayed there for an hour after Ahmaad left. Afraid to move. "T, what's wrong? Why are you so quiet?" Sunny asks her friend. "Hmm? Oh nothing…just got somethings on my mind." Tyra responds. "Like? You holding back from me? Tell me what's up!" Tyra clears her throat and concentrates on the road. "I'm cool Sun, damn. Chill." "Oh no wait a minute bitch. What's up with your tone? You're not ok. Talk to me Tyra." Sunny demands. "I'm in love with you okay! I fucking love you I'm in love with you! And I'm feeling a way about you leaving. So in order for me to deal with this shit

I'm quiet ok!" Tyra yells. "I mean it's not like you give a fuck, right? I mean Sunny only gives a fuck about Sunny. You spin this web of deceit lies and lust to anyone who crosses your path. I've seen you do this shit since we were kids so I know what's up. I just can't believe I'm caught in this shit! You don't know how it feels to want someone you can't have. To want someone so bad you'll do anything just to have a piece of them.

You keep feeding me crumbs and I'm just like a fucking rodent. Sitting around wishing hoping praying you'll drop me a crumb or two to sustain me. I'm sick of feeling this way. Fuck you Sunny! Fuck you for making me fall in love with your ass. And Fuck your crazy ass boyfriend!" Tyra completely lost her shit. Every emotion she had pinned up inside her over the years just erupted like mount Fuji. Sunny was in shock. She knew there was some truth to what Tyra was saying but she wanted Tyra to take responsibility for her part. Anger started to rise in the pit of Sunny's stomach. "You're the one who asked to eat my pussy in your dorm room at Eastern. Or did you forget bitch? I always had a man so what makes my situation any different than what it's always been? Don't you think I care for you too? And if I'm such a piece of shit why are you my friend and why do you keep my pussy in your mouth bitch?" Sunny yells back. "You don't have to worry about that ever again.

I'm done with this bullshit. I wish you all the best but I'm fucking done." Tyra sobs as she pulls down Sunny's mother street. "Fuck you Tyra. Fuck you for abandoning me when I need you the most." Sunny gets out of the car and slams the door. Tyra speeds off. Sunny walks to her car and hears pounding. Her mother is banging on the glass window to get her attention. "Fuck. Now this shit." Sunny mumbles to herself.

"Hey ma, where's my baby?" Sunny's mother looks at Sunny, "We need to talk. Sit down. Now listen Sunny, you're back in good health the trial is behind you. It's time for you to be a mother. You need to get your baby and be his mother. Now I done raised y'all. I'm not raising nothing else. I have helped you as much as I can and I see you going down the wrong path.

You need to clean yourself up and get a job and be this boy's mother. Now you got a good man so don't fuck this up. Aint too many men gonna want you now that you got a baby. So you need to get it together. Caleb can stay here until Sunday. Sunday night you got to get him. Now I love you but baby you need to get your shit together." Sunny looks at her mother through watery eyes. "I got you mom. I appreciate you for helping me out. But I got you."

Sunny gets up and goes to the back where Caleb is sleeping. She picks her son up and all she sees is Ezra. Sunny weeps. Weeps for her son, weeps for herself, weeps for Ezra and the love they once shared. Sunny breaks down as her mother watches through the cracked door. "Mommy misses you so much Caleb. I'm going to be better for you. Mommy is fighting Caleb. Don't give up on me, son. I need you. You're all I have. I love you son. Mommy will be back soon." Sunny kisses her baby boy and puts him back in his crib. She wipes the tears away and straightens her clothes. And just like that Sunny's gone.

Sunny makes a stop at the liquor store before heading home for a pint of Grey Goose. She pulls into her driveway and is thankful to see Ahmaad isn't home. "What a day..." Sunny thinks to herself. There's an envelope taped to the screen door addressed to her. She grabs the envelope and goes inside the house. She pulls off her boots, unbuttons her pants and pours herself a double shot of goose. "What the fuck is this about" She talks to herself. "Dear Sunny, I asked my sister to deliver this to you. I'm sorry. That bullet was meant for me. I'm a lost soul. Please tell my son I love him. I will always love him. I wanted him my entire life. And I'm sorry I failed you both. But I'm at where I should be. I will always love you. I hope you can forgive me one day. For yourself. Not for me because I don't deserve it but you do. I wish you happiness and love. You deserve everything good. I love you Sunny. –E"

Sunny's cheeks are tear stained and her glass is empty. "what the fuck? Where is my goose?" Sunny pours another double shot. She downs it in two gulps. She slams the glass on the kitchen counter and it shatters into dozens of pieces cutting her palm.

"Got damnit!" Sunny yells as she grabs her cut bleeding hand. She walks over to the sink and cuts on the water. She looks out the kitchen window and sees rain drops falling. Lightning dancing in the sky. She grabs the sink and bears down. She screams as loud as she can. She screams again. And again. And again. Finally collapsing onto the cold kitchen floor. Sunny was completely broken.

Reading Ezra's words did something to her. For the first time since she's been shot, she finally allowed herself to feel something besides hatred. She felt Ezra's words penetrate her core. Tyra's words kept ringing in her ears. Her mother's heart to heart was flooding her thoughts. She felt guilty and responsible for everything that's happened to her. "I pushed him to do this and now he doesn't have a life. My son won't ever know his father. I won't ever be in love again. All because of my selfishness. What the fuck is wrong with me? Why me, God? Huh? WHY?" Sunny yells as she throws a plate at the wall. "Sunny, where you at baby?" Ahmaad yells out as he walks into the house. Sunny doesn't say anything. She's caught by surprise. She doesn't have time to hide her tears or the mess she's made in the kitchen. But she has just enough time to stuff the letter down her pants. "Baby what the fuck? What happened to you?" Ahmaad says while rushing to Sunny's side. "Baby you're bleeding everywhere! What happened Sunny?" Ahmaad is almost in a panic. He walks her over to the sink and rinses the wound. He grabs a dish towel and rips it down the middle in two. "I…I was drinking too much I guess. Got a lil emotional and cut my hand on the glass." Sunny whispers. "Got damnit Sun. I got you baby. I got you." Ahmaad says while wrapping Sunny's hand tight. "Come on lets clean you up and I'll get this mess straightened in the kitchen." Ahmaad says. "No baby I just wanna take a bath and go to bed. I don't need help. I just gotta go to bed." Ahmaad reluctantly agrees and helps her to the bathroom and he goes back into the kitchen to clean up the glass and blood. Sunny fishes for a tail in the ashtray on top of the medicine cabinet. She finds a nice size one and lights it along with lighting the letter from Ezra.

The letter is engulfed in flames as Sunny drops it in the toilet. "I love you too E." Sunny whispers as she flushes the toilet. *knock knock* Ahmaad peeks in. "You alright baby?" Ahmaad asks Sunny. "Yeah I just wanted to smoke a lil." Sunny says through a crooked smile. "Alright bae let me know if you need me. We may have to get you stitches if you don't stop bleeding in an hour." Sunny shakes her head okay as Ahmaad closes the door. "What a muthafuckin day." Sunny says to herself through the mirror.

Four weeks has passed since Sunny's melt down. Caleb is back in her care, she cut back on drinking and smoking and she still hasn't spoken to Tyra. It's been a big adjustment for Sunny. Getting back into the grove of motherhood but she's doing it with grace and dignity. She's putting the needs of her son before hers. It seems as if any outside forces that tried to bring her down or derail her from her path has stayed out of her way.

Her focus is definitely all about Caleb and she's trying to distance herself from Ahmaad. "Sunny we need to talk." Says Ahmaad. "About?" Sunny asks. "About us. You, me, this relationship. Everything" Ahmaad yells. "Let me put Caleb down for his nap and we can talk about whatever." Ahmaad storms out of the nursery. He feels like it's just one more person Sunny puts before his needs and he's had enough. He feels rejected and undesirable. He doesn't understand why or how the connection was lost but he wants to do whatever he can to get it back. 30 minutes passed and Sunny emerges from Caleb's room, tiptoeing out the door as to not wake him. Sunny walks past Ahmaad who is sitting on the couch and goes downstairs to get the laundry. She comes back upstairs and into their room and starts folding clothes.

Ahmaad comes in the room about five minutes later. "Are you fucking kidding me right now? What, so now I'm invisible around this muthafucka?" Ahmaad yells. "Shhh! You're going to wake up the baby. What are you even talking about Ahmaad?" Sunny replies seemingly annoyed. "I just told you I wanted to talk. An hour later you come out the baby's room and walk past me and don't say shit then start folding these fucking clothes?!" Ahmaad kicks over the basket of clothes. His feelings are hurt. "What the fuck is wrong with you? I'm around this bitch cooking cleaning raising a baby about to go back to work after I almost lose my fucking life 3 months ago nigga! And you got nerves to say we need to talk about us? What the fuck you want to talk about nigga? I'm listening? Speak got damnit!" Ahmaad looked at Sunny in disbelief. "I don't even know who you are anymore." Says Ahmaad as he grabs his keys and walks out the door. "Finally I got this nigga!" Sunny says as she watches Ahmaad pull off.

She gets on her phone and calls Veronica. "What's up? You need to call him. He will come over. Trust me. Call me right back so I can be on my way." Sunny ends the call. She's been checking in with Veronica once a week. Giving her just enough to keep her around. Veronica's asked Sunny to come over several times despite Sunny rejecting all her advances. Pushing Ahmaad into Veronica's arms has been her plan ever since she took a swim in the Puerto Rican side piece pond. Finally, everything is coming into fruition. Sunny calls her mother to see if she'll watch Caleb. And Veronica text back you have 1 hour before he gets here. Sunny throws everything she thinks Caleb will need into his diaper bag and she rushes out of the house.

She gets to her mom's house in 10 minutes flat. Kisses Caleb and dashes out the door. "I'm finally going to get this nigga once and for all." Sunny zooms down I-94E to get to Veronica's high rise before Ahmaad. She barely makes it. As soon as Veronica buzzes her in Ahmaad pulls up. "Ok listen don't you say a word! Just chill and let me do me." Veronica tells Sunny. "Bitch do you and I'll do me. Ok go go go!" Sunny says as she hides herself in Veronica's hallway closet. "How you doing stranger?" Veronica greets Ahmaad. "I'm cool." "I'm glad you agreed to come over. I've been missing you." Veronica says. "Is that right? Show me how much." Ahmaad says. Sunny hears Ahmaad's belt buckle clanking. She hears his zipper being undone and then she hears moaning and sucking noises. "This bitch is sucking his dick." Sunny puts her hand over her mouth. She's trying to keep her composure. She keeps saying to herself, Sunny you know a hoe can only be a hoe. "Get off my dick. Go get my shit. You know what I want." Ahmaad demands of Veronica. "Yes daddy." Veronica replies.

She comes back with a box of anal sex toys. "Which one you in the mood for today daddy?" I want that plug bitch. And I want you to suck my balls while you do it. Sunny is in disbelief. "A plug? What the fuck is he talking about?" Sunny thought to herself. All you could hear is slurping and moaning from both Veronica and Ahmaad. Sunny opens the closet door as quietly as she could without causing it to creek. She walks down the hall towards Veronica's bedroom. She presses her body firmly against the wall and creeps down the hall. She's finally at the doorway. "Hit that shit harder Bitch! Harder! Grrrr!" Ahmaad yells out in ecstasy. Sunny peeks in and peeks out really fast. "What the fuck?" Sunny says to herself.

She looks again and sees Ahmaad on all fours, his ass tooted up and Veronica is laying on her back under his dick, sucking his balls and fucking his ass with a butt plug. Sunny starts laughing hysterically. Ahmaad jumped what seemed to be 12 feet high. "What the fuck? No! No! Sunny what are you doing? Baby No!" Sunny stops laughing when Ahmaad starts putting his pants on. "Yo, V. You a bad bitch. He's all yours." Sunny says while shaking her head and chucks up the peace sign. "Sunny wait got damnit!" Ahmaad screams out to her. "What the fuck you calling out to her for? Hello? Nigga you got your nerve!" Veronica says to Ahmaad. He doesn't pay her any attention. He's trying to stuff his feet into his shoes before Sunny walks out of the apartment. "Sunny wait!!" Ahmaad yells as he shoves Veronica out of his way. "Nigga, don't fucking push me! I'm pregnant!" Veronica shouts out. Sunny stops dead in her tracks.

She closes the door and walks back inside the apartment. "You're pregnant?" Sunny asks. "She's muthafucka? Are you fucking kidding me?" Sunny says to Ahmaad as she walks towards him. "Sunny it aint mine. I haven't fucked this bitch since you first called me out on it. I haven't touched her called her text her no nothing." Ahmaad pleads. "All of that is true. But I'm four months' pregnant asshole. With your damn baby. We can do a paternity test; I don't give a fuck I know where my pussy been. And it's been in both y'all mouths." Veronica spews. "Shut the fuck up, bitch!" Ahmaad yells. "No you shut the fuck up. Matter of fact both of y'all get out my damn house! You got me fucked up!" Veronica shouts. Before anyone knew it Ahmaad's hands were wrapped around Veronica's neck. He totally blanked out. "Fucking bitch trying to hoe me! Trying to ruin my family you stanking bitch!" Ahmaad says through gritted teeth. "Ahmaad let her go! Let her go! Ahmaad!!" Sunny yells and smacks Ahmaad. He loosens his grip. Veronica goes limp. Ahmaad drops her as if she was hot to touch. He wipes his hands on his shirt. "What the fuck did you just do Ahmaad!" Sunny yells. She walks over to Veronica to check if she's still breathing. "She's just passed out. You better get out of here you fucking dummy. Go!" Sunny yells at Ahmaad. He's shaken up. He doesn't know what he's just done. But he knows if Sunny says go, he has to go. He leaves the apartment. Sunny rummages through Veronica's apartment. She finds the ultrasound pictures taken just two weeks ago with her estimated due date. "This bitch been plotting on me the whole time." She hears Veronica moaning and coughing. She stands over her and watches. Veronica opens her eyes and she jumps up and runs into her bedroom. "I'm calling the police! Get the fuck out of my house!" "Listen Veronica. I'm leaving. You don't want to involve the police. Trust me. He's all yours now. Congratulations you stupid hoe." Sunny says.

She turns on her heels and walks out of the apartment where Ahmaad is waiting for her. "Sunny please get in please talk to me." Ahmaad begs. "Go home Ahmaad. NOW!" Sunny yells. "Man I aint going nowhere until you tell me what the fucks going on! Sunny what was all this huh?" Sunny bites her lower lip and rubs her temples. "She's calling the police my nigga. Think of your future. GO HOME. I will see you there. Fuck!" Sunny says. "Alright I'm going." Ahmaad pulls off.

Sunny sits in her car trying to digest everything that just happened. She can see Veronica looking out of her window so she decides to pull off. Sunny's phone starts ringing nonstop. Calls from both Veronica and Ahmaad. She ignores them and drives to the river front Downtown Detroit. She finds a place to park her car and have full view of the Detroit river. Bodies of water always seem to give her a sense of peace. She stares into the sparkling water and the clear cold evening sky and tears fill her eyes. Her hands grip the steering wheel tighter and tighter. She begins to tremble. Her breathing is fast. "I can't take this shit. I can't fucking take this shit! Why me, God? What did I do to deserve this life? Ever since I've been on this earth all I've known is pain. Is that what you put me here for God? Huh? To be hurt and used! Abused and abandoned? Huh? Well Fuck you! Fuck you God! I've had enough of this shit! Fuck you!!!!" Sunny screams at the top of her lungs. She beats the steering wheel and the roof of the car so violently the car shakes. She sobs for what seemed to be an eternity for her. She climbed in the back seat of her Toyota Camry and cried herself to sleep.

Knock knock knock Sunny is startled. She rubs her eyes and sees a bright flash light shining in her face. She sits up and opens the back door. "Ma'am you can't park here and sleep. You gotta move it. Are you ok?" The DPD officer asked Sunny. "I'm great. Sorry." Sunny said. "You don't look great. You look like you've been crying. Are you sure you're ok to drive?" The officer asks. "Oh my God. What? are you going to arrest me for sleeping in my car? I'm fine! now may I please go? Damn!" The officer looks at Sunny long and hard. "There's no need for the attitude. I'm just making sure you will be safe. I see a lot of heinous shit on the beat so forgive me for giving a fuck about your rude ass. Good day miss." The officer says as he tips his hat and walks back to his squad car. Sunny just rolled her eyes and got into the front seat of her car.

She exhaled loudly and got back out of the car. She walked to the rear of her car where the patrol officer was still parked. She motioned for him to roll his window down. The officer obliged. "Listen, I'm really sorry for being such a bitch. Just having a really shitty day. Thanks for checking on me officer. Be safe." Sunny says remorsefully as she turns on her heels to walk back towards her car. "I'm Calvin. Calvin Jones. I didn't catch your name" Sunny smiled. "Sunny. I'm Sunny, Calvin. Thanks again ok?" "Nothing to thank me for. Just doing my job. But you need to stop fucking with those hoe ass niggas. You'll be a lot happier and stress free." Sunny's eyes popped open. "Excuse me? How do you know I'm upset over a hoe ass nigga?" Sunny says in her high pitch tone. "Am I wrong though?" The officer asks.

They locked eyes and they both laugh. "I know that look. I've seen it a hundred times." The officer replies. "So, that means you aint shit or you're a hoe ass nigga; If you've seen a woman look like I'm looking. How many times have you shitted on her/them? I'm just curious." The officer looks at Sunny sideways, "I'm no bird. I don't shit on anyone. Sunny, I'm a grown ass man. I don't have time for games. If I fuck with you I do if I don't I won't. Simple. Why don't you see for yourself and take my number?" Police officer Calvin suggest. "No thank you. I like living on the edge. My lifestyle goes against your code of ethics. You wouldn't want to blur those lines now would you Mr. Officer of the law?" Sunny says demurely. "You know edge is my middle name." The officer responds. "I bet it is." Sunny rolls her eyes. The officer pulls out his badge and shows Sunny his identification. "Well I'll be damned. Calvin Edge Jones. Edge really is your middle name." Sunny says through giggles. "Yeah so quit bullshitting and take my number down."

Sunny gets her phone out of her back pocket and locks him in. "Alright I gotta go officer edge. I'll be in touch." The officer checks out Sunny's body from head to toe. "Don't make me wait too long Sunshine." Sunny through up her hand gesturing goodbye and she gets in her car. This little exchange actually made her feel better. "I still got it. Imma call his ass tomorrow." Sunny says to herself. She checks her phone and she has over 50 missed calls from both Veronica and Ahmaad. Sunny decides to go home and deal with her reality.

Sunny can't even get inside the house good without Ahmaad rushing to the door to open it. "Sunny I've been calling you for hours. Please let me explain myself." Ahmaad begs. "Ahmaad sit down. Just sit down and listen." Ahmaad does what he's told. "I'm not doing this. I could've maybe handled the fact that you fucked another bitch. But the way she fucks you and the fact you got a baby on the way is too much. So I don't know if you're gay, you just like gay sex, or what. I don't know any niggas who likes to be fucked in the ass by their bitch. So I get why you stepped out on me. Because I didn't fuck you the way you liked. So now you don't have to hide or feel deprived anymore. You can be free and do what you please and get fucked in your ass by whomever you please. I can't believe you deceived me for so long. We'll be out of here by the weekend." Sunny gets up and goes to the nursery and starts packing up Caleb's things. "So you're not going to hear anything I have to say? Do you know what I've sacrificed to be with you?" Ahmaad yells. "Did I ask you to sacrifice anything for me nigga? I didn't ask you for shit. If you want to talk to me, you going about it wrong. I don't care to hear whatever the fuck you gotta say." Sunny yells back.

Sunny continues to pack. Ahmaad is pacing the floor and rubbing his head with his hands out of frustration. He punches the wall creating a huge crater. "No need for none of that. You did this to yourself." Sunny says calmly. "You act like you're so fucking innocent. You got nerve to call me gay when you're carrying on a fucking lesbian affair with your so called bestie. I didn't say shit. I knew why you did it and I accepted it for what it was. I forgave you. And you telling me you can't give me the same chance? After everything we been through?" Sunny rolls her eyes and cocks her head to the side and starts pointing in Ahmaad's face. "See this is why I can't fuck with you. You won't even be real with me. So you just gonna neglect the fact that you put a gun to Tyra's head, huh? You so afraid of being exposed for the psychopath you are you're holding on to this Character Ahmaad for dear life. Let that fake nigga go and be you. Yeah I got my pussy ate so what. It was only when we were going through some bullshit. I'm not saying I'm right but you can't compare what you've done to what I've done. I just want you to get some fucking help. I'm done Ahmaad. I will never trust you. Ever." Sunny's voice quivers and she starts crying. She couldn't hold in her emotions anymore. Ahmaad grabs her by the arms, "Sunny you can't leave me. You are my soul mate Sun. We can work through this shit. I can't lose you and Caleb. I just can't." Sunny struggles to get out of Ahmaad's hold "Let me go Maad. Let me go!" Ahmaad holds on tighter and he starts sobbing. "Sunny I can't. Please baby I can't. I might as well kill myself. I can't lose y'all. Y'all are a part of me. I need my family. I ain't shit without y'all Sunny." Sunny starts to soften.

She becomes less tense and she puts her arms around Ahmaad which made him cry even more. "Please let me make it up to you Sunny. Please?" Ahmaad pleads for his woman. I just don't see how we can ever fix this Ahmaad. I'm going to want to cheat on you anytime you walk out the door because I don't trust you and I refuse to be the only one played. And furthermore I don't even know if you're gay or not!" Ahmaad takes his hands off Sunny and points his pinky in her face, "Stop with that gay shit. I maybe kinky but I'm far from gay. I don't want a dick in my ass. I don't want no nigga dick rubbing on me." Sunny smacks her lips, "So you just want a plastic dick fucking your asshole? What's the difference Ahmaad? I mean really." "it's a big fucking difference. This one of the reasons I kept Veronica around because she into kinky shit like I like. It's been my experience that when I'm with a black woman and she finds out what I like sexually she labels me gay. But why should you have all the fun? I should be able to enjoy sex and have it how I want it without being labeled or judged. You like eating pussy. I saw that punk ass video. You ate the shit out Tyra's pussy. So are you gay now? Alright then. Don't do me." Ahmaad makes his case. "ok, even still if I can forgive all that. I'm not forgiving no baby. I'm just not. And I'm definitely not dealing with you and your baby mamas relationship." Sunny says emphatically. "Sunny it's not my baby." "Nigga you sound foolish. You won't know until you take that damn test. Don't act like you didn't fuck her raw before." Ahmaad looks at Sunny with blood shot red eyes and quivering lips. "Sunny I can't have kids. It's not my fucking child." Sunny is confused. "What do you mean you can't have kids, Ahmaad.? Hello? Answer me!" Ahmaad goes into the kitchen and pulls the fifth of Hennessy out the freezer.

He pours himself and Sunny a double shot. He gulps the double shot and slam the glass down on the kitchen counter. "I was raped as a kid Sunny. I was raped and beaten half to death by my stepdad when I was 8 years old. The injuries I sustained caused me to be unable to produce children." Ahmaad pours another drink. Sunny is in shock. Her head is spinning. "Ahmaad why didn't you tell me? I mean we've talked about having kids. You lied to me, again? Ahmaad I don't even know you. I'm so sorry that happened to you Ahmaad but why? Why didn't you just tell me? You know what happened to me as a child so why wouldn't you feel compelled to share what happened to you?" Ahmaad starts rolling a blunt. "Because I'm a man Sunny. What man wants to admit to being raped and can't have kids? Everything that makes a man a man that muthafucka took from me. He stole it! And here comes you…the woman of my dreams. Then I find out you're pregnant. I felt it was meant to be. This would be my chance to feel like a father. Caleb will only know me as his father since I caught him out the pussy okay. You gave me my manhood back. Something I never thought would happen for me Sun." Ahmaad voice trembles. He's fighting back his tears. "Come here Ahmaad. Baby come here." Sunny tries to embrace him but he refuses. "No. I don't want to hug. I'm fucked up Sunny. I've never told anyone this. My mother and uncles know but I've never told any friends or girlfriends for sure. So excuse me for not wanting to hug right now. I feel like a bitch." "Baby don't say that! I'm your woman, I'm supposed to be your best friend. You should feel like more of a man for sharing such a horrific tragedy that's happened to you. I hate that I had to find out like this but got damnit Maad."

The couple sit on the couch and stare at the ceiling while passing the blunt and Hennessey back and forth to each other. "What a fucking mess we are Ahmaad. A beautiful mess. Sunny scoots closer to Ahmaad and lays her head into his chest. "I can't lose you Sun. I don't know what I'll do." Ahmaad says as one tear fell from his right eye. Sunny wiped his tear from his cheek. "I'm not going anywhere Ahmaad. But we need counseling. And I need some time to figure things out. But I don't want to leave you okay. I want to try but I need some time to clear shit out my head." "Ok baby, I just have to accept that. Take all the time you need just don't leave me bae. Just don't." Sunny grabs Ahmaad's face and puts her forehead against his, "I love you Maady. We going to figure this shit out. But I need you to call your doctor in the morning and make an appointment to get checked for any and all STD's thank you very much and I will do the same. And don't even think of touching me until we take care of this." Sunny says firmly. "I can't even eat it, bae?" Ahmaad asks almost whining. "No. You can't even sniff it." Ahmaad pours himself another drink, "If I want to eat that pussy I'm eating it. Have another shot." Ahmaad says matter of factly.

6

It's been a week and a half since everything broke out about Ahmaad and Veronica. Sunny has been trying to forgive and forget but she can't get the image of Ahmaad being fucked in the ass out of her head. She doesn't even find him attractive sexually anymore. She has no one to talk to since Tyra was her only real friend she felt comfortable sharing things with. "Baby the doc called and said I have a clean bill of health. Did they call you?" Ahmaad asks. "Um no. I'll call them in a minute." Sunny says annoyed. "What's up your butt?" Ahmaad asks while pinching Sunny's cheeks. "Don't say anything about a butt to me." Sunny replies snarky. "What in the hell is that supposed to mean?"

Sunny rolls her eyes, "Nothing. I'm just having a moment." Ahmaad sits next to Sunny in the kitchen while she's feeding Caleb mashed potatoes. "Talk to me Sun." "Ahmaad, I don't understand this ass sex. I legit look at you different. It's fucking with me. " Ahmaad gets up and pushes his chair in. "After I poured my heart out to you this what you do? You throw this shit in my face like this and in front of our son? If I was gay, I would let a man fuck me with your ignorant ass. Just because I don't have limits with whatever bitch I decide to fuck doesn't make me gay. I don't want a fucking nigga. I want pussy only." Ahmaad's tone is abrasive. "Pussy with a side of dildo in your ass though? Oh ok. Yeah that's normal." Sunny says with an attitude while shoving spoonful of mashed potatoes to baby Caleb.

Ahmaad snatches the bowl of mashed potatoes

from Sunny and he hurls it at the wall causing mashed potatoes to color the wall and Sunny's hair. Ahmaad gets in Sunny's face and points his index finger, "Let that be the last fucking time you ever disrespect me, bitch. And I mean it." Ahmaad says in such a scary and threatening tone. Sunny knew not to say anything. She was afraid. Ahmaad's never called her out of her name and he's never gotten in her face like this. Ahmaad grabbed his jacket and keys and slammed the door behind him. Baby Caleb starts crying. Sunny picks up the baby and consoles him. "Mommy sorry Caleb, Mommy sorry. Daddy is an idiot. Well Ahmaad is an idiot. Not daddy. You wanna take a bath with mommy? Huh? Yeah? Let's take a bath, yay!" Sunny says to her son while he stops crying and coos and laughs in delight at his mother's voice.

Sunny runs a bath for she and Caleb. Caleb sits

in between his mom's legs trying to eat the bubbles and put them in his hair. Sunny gets a text message from Ezra's sister. It simply says 'did you get the letter?' Sunny thought better than to text back. She didn't want to leave any evidence behind that she speaks to Ezra's family or that he's trying to make contact. She decides to call him.

"What's up Stacy. Yeah I got it so what does he want exactly?" Sunny asks trying to sound uninterested. "Sunny, he's just trying to atone for everything. This whole situation is fucked and what's really hurting us is we don't have a relationship with Caleb. I understand the seriousness of this situation. My brother tried to kill you. He left you for dead. It's unforgivable. But we don't want to be punished for his sins. My brother will probably spend the rest of his life in jail and Caleb is all we have of him. He probably won't have another child. He wants you to find it in your heart to pay him a visit so he can tell you face to face about how sorry he is for everything. He put you on his list to visit so I'm just doing what I told him I would do and that is talk to you." Stacey says a mouthful. "Um...wow. This is a lot to digest Stacey. Just give me some time and we'll figure something out about Caleb. I need time Stacey." Sunny says. Stacey agrees with Sunny and she ends the call. She sinks back in the tub and cradles her baby tightly as she sobs.

Ahmaad returns home to find Sunny asleep on the floor in the nursery. Ahmaad knew he fucked up. He felt defeated. He sits on the floor in the hallway and watches Sunny and Caleb sleep until he fell into his own slumber.

Morning breaks and Sunny is getting herself and baby Caleb ready to head out. Ahmaad is awakened by Caleb cooing. "Good morning guys." Ahmaad says. “Morning” Sunny responds dryly. “I apologize Sunny. I was wrong and I shouldn’t have ever disrespected you. I feel like I’m losing you Sun. I don’t know what to do.” Sunny doesn’t stop getting Caleb dressed nor does she make eye contact.

“I told you Ahmaad I need time. Just give me time and space.” Ahmaad sighs, “Alright Sunny. Alright. Where are you going? Can I still know where you go when you leave our home or not?” Ahmaad asks sarcastically. Sunny rolls her eyes. “Caleb is going over my parents and I have errands to run.” “Alright, well maybe we can go to lunch if you’re free?” Ahmaad asks. “We’ll see. I’ll text you.” Ahmaad shakes his head and gets himself ready for work. Sunny is out the door before he gets out of the shower.

Sunny drops off Caleb to her parents and she heads to Saginaw Correctional facility to see Ezra.

She arrives two hours later. "What the fuck bitch? Why am I here? What am I doing? Fuuuuuck!!" Sunny talks to herself through the visor mirror. She pops a molly and waits until she feels the affects. She reclines her car seat back and tries to calm her breathing down. She starts to see starburst and her legs begin to tingle. She grabs her bottle of Evian and downs it in less than 30 seconds. "Damn I'm high as fuck. Ok, let's do this." Sunny says to herself while she checks her makeup. It takes her a little over an hour before she gets into the visitation room. She sees a vending machine and gets a pack of gum and an apple juice. The big metal door opens and she hears shackles. The C.O.'s are bringing the inmates out. Ezra is at the front of the line. Sunny almost drops her juice but she sat down instead. She felt flushed and hot.

Ezra's looking around the room trying to figure out

who's here to see him. He and Sunny lock eyes. His eye's get as big as half dollars. "I can't believe you're here. I'm grateful you are. I can't believe this though. Thank you for coming." Sunny regains her composure. "There's nothing to thank me for. I'm doing this for me and my son. Not you." Sunny gets Caleb's picture from her back pocket and gives it to Ezra. He silently sobs. "He's a good baby and very smart and loving. You're really missing out on an amazing person. I need to know why, Ezra. Why?" Ezra shifts in his seat and rubs his sweaty palms on his orange jumpsuit. "Sunny I lost my mind. That's all I can say is I lost my mind. I felt like if I couldn't have you nobody could. I couldn't eat sleep function. Every thought was you and Caleb. I was going mad. So I did what I did. That's as plain as I can put it." Sunny becomes enraged. Her legs start to shake her cheeks turn red.

She has sweat beads along her forehead. "You shot me and left me for dead like a fucking animal. I hope you rot in this bitch!" Sunny says while grinding her teeth. Ezra never breaks his stare. "I understand Sunny. Believe me I do. There's no excuse." They both sit in silence for what seemed to be an eternity. Staring into each other's eyes. Sunny calms down and her legs stop shaking. "You're so beautiful Sunny. Are you happy?" Ezra asks. "Very. And satisfied." Sunny replies with one eyebrow raised. Ezra clears his throat and fidgets. "That makes me happy.... That you're happy. You and Caleb. That's it." Sunny chuckles. "Do you miss my pussy?" Without missing a beat, "Every fucking day of my life. You're all I masturbate to." Sunny smiles, "Good." They continue to stare in silence. "Times up visitors.!" The guard shouts. "Thank you Sunny. I will always love you." Sunny grabs Ezra's hand and puts it down the front of her pants. He fumbles around and slips his middle finger inside her pussy just before the guard notices. "Ay ay ay! No we're not doing that!" the guard shouts. "Fuck you Ezra. FUCK YOU." Sunny says while walking away from him. The guards whisk Ezra back to his cell as Sunny heads out of the prison back to her car. It was as if she held her breath the entire walk because when she finally got inside her car she let out the longest sigh and scream.

"Ahhhhhhhhhh!!!! I hate that nigga! I hate him!" Sunny screams while hitting her steering wheel. She hits the roof of her car with her fists. She puts her head in her hands and starts crying. "Why do I love him still? Why do I feel like this God? Why? Answer me got damnit!" Sunny sits in her car for an hour trying to collect her thoughts and compose herself for the two-hour drive home. She looks at her phone and she's missed Ahmadis phone calls.

He sent a text that read, "I guess that's a no for lunch." She tosses her phone in the passenger seat and drives home. Sunny was grateful for the two-hour drive. It gave her time to think about what she needed to do why she makes the decisions she makes and how she vows to never let anyone get close enough to her to hurt her, again. She decided she's going to strike first. She grabs her phone and decides to make a call. "How are you stranger?" She says. "I'm aight who is this?" The caller responds. "Sunny." There's a 5 second pause. "Little miss sunshine. I was beginning to think you wouldn't call. Glad you came to your senses. So what up wit chu? You been sleeping at the river front lately?" Officer Calvin jokes. "You're such an asshole. This is the only reason I like you a little bit." Sunny responds. "Oh so you like me? Yesss! Since you liking me lets grab a bite and some dranks tonight?" Sunny takes

Calvin up on his offer. Sunny pulls up at home and Ahmaad isn't there. "Good, I hope his ass stays gone until I dip." Sunny showers, shaves her pussy and legs, puts on her Chanel perfume Ahmaad gave her for Christmas and she squeezes into the tightest black mini skirt she owns with a pair of black suede thigh high boots and a black body suit with cut outs on her shoulders baring her tattoos. She accessorizes with large gold hoop earrings, a gold chain with a crucifix drenched in diamonds also gifted by Ahmaad and gold bangles on her wrist. Her hair is flowing down her back with wavy curls looking like a black Farrah Fawcett. She takes one last look at herself before putting on her coat. "Damn I look good." She hears Ahmaad coming into the house. "Fuck. I don't have time for this fag ass nigga."

Sunny puts on her coat grabs her purse and heads for the door. "Whoa…where are we going?"

Ahmaad asks. Sunny remains silent. "Ok then where are YOU going, Sunny?" "Out. I'm going out. Don't wait up." Sunny responds while looking for her keys. "Hold the fuck up. You got me twisted if you think I'm going to allow this shit to go on. Where in the fuck are you going Sunny? You got your pussy hanging out, smelling like you're ready to fuck. You're still my woman." Sunny sighs and rolls her eyes. "Ahmaad was I your woman when you were getting fucked in your ass by Veronica? Huh? Yeah I didn't think so. I'm going out. I don't know where. I'm going by myself. I want to have a drink and a good time without being reminded of how fucked up my life is right now, okay?" Ahmaad eyes turned black. He grabs Sunny by her neck and starts choking her. "Didn't I tell you not to disrespect me like that again? I told you didn't I? huh?!" Sunny is unable to speak. Ahmaad's grip is too strong. She's clawing at his hands drawing blood trying to get him to release his grip, but she's unsuccessful.

Ahmaad drags her into the dining room and throws Sunny onto the dining room table face first. Her tooth cuts into her bottom lip from the impact of the throw. "Get off me! Get the fuck off me!! Stop it! Stop!" Sunny screams out. Ahmaad pins Sunny down by the back of her neck. He hikes up her mini-skirt and rips her thong panties in one swipe. He fumbles around with the button and zipper on his jeans and he pulls out his semi hard dick. "Get the fuck off me! Ahmaad stop! Noooooo! What are you doing?! Stop it!" Sunny pleads. Ahmaad doesn't hear anything. He's in rage mode. He spits on his free hand and rubs the spit over the head of his dick really fast and rams his dick inside of Sunny. Sunny goes numb. She stops fighting him. She relaxes her body and he rapes her.

She stares out the window with her face mashed against the wooden dining room table with tears pooling under her cheek. She goes into another place in her mind. Another dimension. Somewhere deep inside where she feels safe. Where no one can touch her. No one. Ahmaad thrusts 6 times before ejaculating inside her. He pulls his semen covered dick out and stuffs it back into his pants. He's out of breath and collapses against the wall. Sunny gets up and goes into the bathroom. She gets her wash rag and suds it up washing any traces of Ahmaad, off her vagina. Her lips are bloodied. She wipes the blood from her lips and mouth. She washes the tears from her face and reapplies her mascara, puts on some red lipstick and heads out the door. Ahmaad is sobbing on the floor with his back against the wall and his head hanging low like a wounded coward. Sunny steps over him, grabs her keys and purse and heads out the door.

"I need some weed. Let me call Dre. Dre what's up I need to grab something from you. Are you home? Alright bet I'm on my way. Lemme get a half eighth. See you in a minute." Sunny arrives at Dre's house, the drug dealer she met through Tyra. "Damn girl. Where you going looking like you looking?" Dre says while adjusting his dick inside his boxer because he got an instant erection looking at Sunny all dolled up. Unable to detect that less than 30 minutes ago she was raped by the man she calls her boyfriend. "Just scooting and booting. Lemme get that though." Sunny says. "Oh you must be going to see a nigga the way you rushing me. He better be hitting that right and paying all your muthafuckin bills, the way you looking." Sunny raises her left eyebrow and bites her bottom lip seductively. "And if he aint are you saying you can hit it better?"

Dre steps back and rubs his goatee. "I can show you better." Dre replies. Sunny walks up on Dre being sure to keep eye contact. She grabs his dick through his jeans. Dre doesn't budge. "Mmm you do like what you see, huh?" Sunny says while rubbing his erect penis through his jeans. "See, now don't start something you can't finish. You fucking with a real nigga." Sunny snickers. She unbuttons his pants. "I want to see what a real nigga dick looks like. Show me." Sunny asks. Dre starts laughing showing his bright white teeth and his deep dimples on both cheeks. He unzips his pants and lets them hit the floor. Sunny doesn't break eye contact. "Pull your boxers down slowly." Dre stops laughing. His penis is fully erect now.

Sunny is in control and he's completely turned on. Without saying a word Dre slowly pulls his boxers down showing off his oblique's. His pubic hairs peek out from the brim of his boxers. He continues to slide them off slowly exposing every inch of his body. Sunny gets excited. "Stop. Don't move." Sunny says while walking over to his lazy boy chair. "Girl what are you doing? What you got me over here doing?" "Stop talking. You said you can show me better. Show me. Now take your boxers off. Slow." Sunny says as she sits comfortably in his lazy boy while draping her leg over the arm of the chair exposing her bald pussy. Dre's mouth is hanging open while doing exactly what Sunny told him to do. His boxers slid over his dick causing it to spring up slapping itself against his stomach. Dre had the biggest dick Sunny's ever seen. It had to be at least 11 inches. Strong possibility of 12. "I guess you do got a real nigga dick. Show me how a real nigga jacks off." Dre starts laughing. "Naw ma, real niggas don't jack off we get jacked off. Come jack it off for me. Don't be scared."

Sunny puts her two fingers inside her pussy. She moves them in and out in and out. She pulls her fingers out from inside her creamy center and looks at them. She spreads her index and middle finger apart causing a string of pussy juice to stretch between the two like a bridge. She puts her fingers inside her mouth and licks them clean. "Dre, I thought you were a real nigga. Tsk tsk. Look how wet you got me without even touching me. I want to see if you can make me cum just by watching you jack that big ass dick for me, baby." Sunny says while rubbing her clit. Dre was game. He was so turned on by Sunny sitting there on his lazy boy with her thigh highs and her masturbating for him. "damn girl. You got me tripping." Dre says while relinquishing his pride by taking his dick in his hand and stroking it up and down slowly but steady. Causing veins to pop out of his forearms and shaft. "Faster. Stroke it faster." Sunny demands. Dre does exactly that. Sunny starts moaning as her clit swells from her finger tips rubbing ferociously against her clit. "Now spit on it Dre. Spit on your dick for me baby. Fuck!" Sunny asks while panting and quivering as she approaches her climax. Dre puts his hand against the wall for balance. He looks down at his dick and spits on the head. He rims the head with his hand spreading his saliva around making his dick look like a well-oiled black steel pipe. Dre stares at Sunny intensely while picking up the speed of his stroke. Sunny is moaning and calling his name. "Dre, are you really about to make me cum? Dre? Baby I'm about to cum!" Sunny says through breaths. "Cum for a real nigga then Suuunnnnnneeeeee!" Dre says as his nut squirts across his carpeted floor.

Sunny cums simultaneously after seeing his

sperm shoot out like a super soaker across the living room floor. "Damn…You're trouble for me Dre." Sunny says while standing up pulling her mini skirt down and gathering herself. She walks over to him who is now sitting on the couch naked and his dick is still hard. She straddles him and leans into his ear, "Let me get that bag so I can dip." Sunny gets up and looks at Dre intently. Dre chuckles, "Alright. Alright I see what you about. You like to tease niggas. Sunny you a muthafucka" Dre says while stepping into his boxers and going to the back of his apartment to get his product. He comes back with a half eight, "That'll be 30 dollars." Dre says. Sunny smirks and hands him a 50, "Keep the change." Sunny grabs her weed and heads out the door. She rolls up as soon as she gets inside the car and smokes the entire blunt before pulling off. Sunny feels as if she's watching a movie of herself. A total out of body experience. She calls

Calvin and lets him know she's on her way to meet him at the bar. She finishes the last shot of Hennessy she had in her car and hits the freeway.

Sunny arrives at the bar and before she gets out she grabs some wipes from her glove box and wipes her vagina to freshen it up. She puts hand sanitizer on her hands and rubs vigorously. She grabs her Chanel perfume and sprays it in her hair, behind her knees, in between her thighs and her cleavage. She grabs her Binaca spray and freshens her breath. She checks her makeup and hair and now she's ready to meet officer Calvin. She stumbles when she first gets out of the car but quickly recovers. "Get it together, bitch."

Sunny says to herself while walking to the bar. Calvin had been watching Sunny from his car. He was in the parking lot waiting and decide to watch Sunny before letting her know he was there. He gets out of his car and catches up with her. "Funny meeting you here lil lady." Calvin whispers in Sunny's ear. She spun around and hit Calvin in his shoulder. "Boy don't scare me like that! That's how niggas end up on the first 48." Calvin laughs, "Damn you shooting already? Put the guns away ma'am I don't want no trouble. You looking mighty fine, let me get this door for you. "Thank you, Officer." Sunny says sarcastically. Calvin gets a table for the pair to give them a bit more privacy. "So what we drinking tonight?" Calvin asks. "Hennessy of course, darling." Sunny says in a terrible British accent. Calvin orders a Hennessy and a double shot of Jack for himself and tells the waitress to keep them coming. She called him by his name so Sunny assumed this is a cop bar or he just frequents it with his hoes. "Damn they got you on payroll here?" Sunny asks. Calvin laughs,

"Naw I'm just a regular and they take care of their

customers. So what's your deal? What's your story?" Calvin asks. Sunny furrows her eyebrows and shifts in her seat. "Um, I don't have a story. I'm just Sunny." Calvin shakes his head, "Not good enough. I won't allow you to dodge this question. First of all, let's toast. To friendship and honesty. Cheers?" Sunny says "Salud" The pair swallow their drinks in one gulp and slam their shooters on the table. "Ok so my story…I'm a single mom. Getting out of a relationship. Trying to get back into school. I love music. I'm a Gemini and pink is my favorite color. Now your turn." Calvin rubs his chin. The waitress brings another shot of Jack and Hennessy. "So you not gonna talk about being shot and almost dying?" Calvin asks while picking up his drink and raising it in the air waiting for Sunny to join him. She looks at him with squinted eyes.

She grabs her drink and chugs. "So what are you

a stalker now? You doing background checks on me? That's pretty fucking rude." "Rude? I can see how you would feel that way. But at the end of the day I'm a cop. This is my career. I have to know who I'm dealing with at all times you know. We don't have to talk about it but I want you to know that I know. And I also know that you're at your limit right now. I saw you in your car doing your ritual. Trying to mask the weed scent and the alcohol on your breath." Sunny starts to laugh out of nervousness. "Wow you got a lot of fucking nerve. You know what. This was a mistake. A big mistake. I'm going to go. Thanks for the drinks." Sunny says while getting up from the table and walking to the door. Calvin is on her heels as she walks out of the bar. "Sunny wait up!" Calvin yells out. "No, I'm good. You enjoy your night." Sunny says while walking towards her car not even turning around to look at Calvin. Calvin follows Sunny to her car. “Okay wait. I apologize. I’m an asshole and abrasive and intrusive. I don’t play games I get right to the meat. It’s just how I am but I don’t want you to feel disrespected or picked apart. It’s just my way. And for that I am sorry.” Sunny cheeks turn red. She’s shifting her weight by swaying side to side. “The meat huh? So what you wanna know, Calvin? You wanna know about my baby daddy shooting me because I left him for another nigga when I was 5 months pregnant with his baby? You wanna know that I visited him in jail and that I’m still in love with him? You wanna know that my boyfriend might be crazier and more dangerous than my baby daddy is? You wanna know that he raped me tonight? You wanna know that I have to get high and drunk every day to cope? Is this what you want? Well there you go! Now what? Can I go now?”

Sunny says while yelling causing a scene and

onlookers to stop and take a front seat. But Calvin didn't run. He didn't shout. He let Sunny get it out. He felt pity for Sunny. He wanted to help her. "Is that it? Girl I thought you were going to tell me some earth shattering shit. Now can we go get something to eat? Or maybe even coffee?" Sunny was thrown off. "What?" Calvin takes her hand, "A man's gotta eat. Look we can walk right up the street to this Greek restaurant. Best food ever to soak up liquor. What do you say?" Calvin asks. Sunny is hesitant, "ok fine. I can eat." Calvin holds onto Sunny's hand while walking to the restaurant. "Now that, that's out the way we can have a little fun." Calvin says while nudging Sunny with his shoulder. Sunny giggles reluctantly but thinks to herself 'what the fuck is up with this nigga.' They order their food and the energy is much more light. Sunny scarfs down her food as if she hasn't eaten in two days.

Sunny didn't talk much she just listened to Calvin and laughed the entire time. He told the funniest stories about his experiences on the beat and he was genuinely a funny guy. Sunny forgot about all of her problems during dinner. She hasn't laughed this hard this much since before she was shot. It felt good. "It's getting late. I should be getting home. Thank you for this Calvin. You have no idea how much I needed this." Calvin smiles and taps her hand. "It was my pleasure. But before I walk you back to your car, I need to know are you safe there and if not you don't have to be there especially not tonight." "I'm cool. Everything will be fine. I said too much but I need you to know I know how to handle myself. Thank you for asking." Sunny responds. "Alright. Let's get you to your car then."

Calvin pays for their dinner and walks Sunny back to her car. He grabs her hand and kisses it. "Farewell my lady. Safe travels and thanks for laughing at my corn ball jokes." Sunny giggles again. "I like corn ball jokes. Thank you for making a shitty night turn into one of the better ones I've had in a long time. Goodnight Calvin." "Goodnight Sunny." Sunny gets in her car and starts the engine. She watches Calvin get inside his car. She calls him on her cell phone. "Did you forget something?" Calvin asks on the receiving end. "I don't wanna go home." Sunny says. "Well, you wanna come over my house? We can play some cards or something." Calvin asks. "Lead the way." Sunny replies and ends the phone call and Follows Calvin to his house which is oddly 4 blocks from Sunny and Ahmaads house in Redford. Sunny assumed Calvin knew this already so she just kept her mouth closed.

His house was a typical bachelors pad. He was messy but not nasty. Empty Modelo beer glasses lined his kitchen counter and kitchen floor. His dirty uniform was strewn across his couch. Shoes piled up at the door. The smell of weed and incense filled the air. "Excuse the mess. I'm a man so there." Sunny shakes her head, "Yeah you clearly are. So I see you smoke. Let's blow." Sunny says. Calvin just laughs and goes in the back to grab his stash. They smoked two blunts of O.G. Cush and played 7 hands of Tonk. Sunny only won one hand. "You know you're a damn cheater. I'm never playing cards with you again. Fucking cheater. And where are the snacks in this man hole?" "Girl I'm living raw over here. I eat big macs and fruit loops every day. Some fruit loops sound good as hell right now. Want some?" Calvin asks. "Hell yeah!" The two eat fruit loops and laugh until their face hurts while sitting in the middle of the living room floor.

Sunny feels comfortable enough to scoot close to

Calvin and rest her head on his shoulder. Calvin rest his head on top of hers. "Did he do that to your lip?" Calvin whispers to Sunny. Sunny shakes her head yes. "I'm sorry Sunny." Calvin says while gripping her hand. Something inside of Sunny started to bubble over. She couldn't control her emotions. She started to cry. The day's events caught up to her and she unloaded it all unto Calvin's shoulder. She cried so much her body shook. Calvin didn't say a word he just held her in his arms. Sunny started to calm down and she kissed him on his neck. He didn't respond. She kissed him again and nibbled his ear. "Sunny lets get you to bed. Let's lay you down and get a lil nap in." Calvin says. "Lay down with me. Lay with me Calvin. Make me feel good." Sunny asks seductively through tears and lust while still kissing and nibbling on his neck and ear.

Calvin is getting turned on but he knows Sunny is

fragile and he can't possibly sleep with her in good conscience while she's in this state. "Sunny, Sunny as much as I would love to now isn't the right time. Just try to rest your eyes a while. Come on I'll even rest my eyes with you." Sunny buries her head in his chest. "Oh now you wanna be a gentleman. You don't have to be that way with me." Calvin grabs Sunny's chin and lifts her head until her eyes meet his, "Any man should be that way with you, Sunny." Sunny relaxed her entire body and nestled herself into Calvin's chest and arms and fell fast asleep.

The sun peeked into the living room window of Calvin's home. Sunny heard the birds chirping outside. She thought she was home until she looked around and didn't see anything familiar. She was alone tucked under two blankets on Calvin's living room floor. She smelled coffee and bacon. "Good morning sleeping beauty. You want some breakfast?"

Calvin asks. "Uh no. No thank you. Uh listen thanks for everything. You were really sweet. I was a complete mess yesterday so I appreciate.... everything. I'm gonna get outta here." Sunny says while trying to keep her balance while slipping her legs into her thigh high boots. "It was my pleasure Sunny. Maybe next weekend we can catch a movie or something. No pressure." Sunny smiles, "That would be nice. See you later, Calvin." "After while." Calvin says as he walks Sunny to the door and watches her pull off.

7

Ahmaad is still home when Sunny returns. He is sitting on the living room couch. Blood shot eyes and the same clothes from yesterday. Sunny didn't even make eye contact with him. She goes straight to her room and starts packing.

Ahmaad comes in the room and watches her pack in silence. She goes into the baby's room and packs as much as she could. She starts loading up her car with suitcases and baby toys. Ahmaad stood in the hallway in silence watching the love of his life leave him. He felt defeated. Sunny went back in for the final bag and Ahmaad wasn't in the hallway anymore. She took the house key off her key chain, "Your keys are on the kitchen counter. I'll be back for my things later on in the week. Ahmaad? Ahmaad?!" Sunny yells out. Ahmaad didn't respond to her. Sunny walks back into the room and doesn't see him. She heard a noise in the basement. As if something fell over. 'Ahmaad?!" She calls out but no response. Sunny looks in the bathroom and didn't see him. She walks down the basement steps, "Ahmaad what the fuck?" Sunny calls out in aggravation. She turns on the basement lights when she reaches the bottom of the stairs.

There's Ahmaad, hanging from the light fixture. Twitching. Gasping for air with a noose around his neck tightening every second that passes. His feet are searching for the chair he kicked over. "No!!! No!! No!! Ahmaad!!" Sunny runs over to Ahmaad and lifts him by his legs but she's unsuccessful. His weight is too heavy for her small frame. She doesn't want to let go afraid if she does his neck may snap. She sees the chair and grabs it with her foot. She sits the chair upright and tries to plant Ahmaad's feet on the seat so she can get him down. His legs are limp. "Hold on Ahmaad! I'm going to get you down baby! Hold on!" Sunny runs up the steps 3 at a time. She rips open the kitchen drawer causing the flatware to fly all over the kitchen floor. She sees a knife and grabs it.

She practically jumps all of the stairs and twists her ankle. She can't feel it because her adrenaline is pumping. Ahmaad's body is lifeless. Swinging back and forth. Sunny climbs on top of the chair and saws the cable cord from which Ahmaad is hanging. She cuts through the last bit of cabled and they both fall to the ground. Sunny turns Ahmaad onto his back and starts doing chest compressions. She stops and feels his neck for a pulse. She feels his skin beating against her fingertips. "Ahmaad baby wake up! Come back to me Ahmaad wake up!" Sunny runs back upstairs grab her phone and runs back downstairs to call 911. Ahmaad starts coughing while Sunny is talking to the emergency operator. "He's breathing! He's coughing ma'am! Please hurry up please! Come on baby wake up! Come back to me Maad you can't leave me!" Ahmaad opens his eyes. He sees Sunny. She looks angelic.

She has this glow around her and everything else is fuzzy. He doesn't know if he's dead or dreaming. "Sunny? Don't go." Ahmaad says in a raspy whisper. "I'm right here baby. I'm right here! Ma'am he's talking! please where is the ambulance?" *boom boom boom* Loud knocks at the door. The 911 operator tells Sunny it's the emergency responders at the door. Sunny dashes upstairs and lets them in. She takes them downstairs to assess Ahmaad. They ask Sunny to go back upstairs and speak with the officer. Sunny does what they ask. She tells the officer she thinks he did this because she was leaving him. The officer asked why they broke up but Sunny didn't say what Ahmaad did to her. She just says he did somethings that she didn't want to put up with and decided to leave him. Thirty minutes later, Ahmaad walks upstairs with the paramedics and what looks to be burn marks around his neck from the cable he hung himself with.

He's refusing to go to the hospital. "Sir, we can't make you go but it seems as if you may need some help buddy. Life should never get this bad and if it does it's okay to get help. This is why we're here. Let us help you buddy." The officer pleads with Ahmaad. Ahmaad can barely speak because the cable bruised his vocal cords. "I told myself if I wake up and I'm still alive it's not my time. No matter if she leaves me or stays. It's not my time." Ahmaad rubs the front of his neck and tears stream down his face. Sunny starts to cry. The officer leaves behind pamphlets and phone numbers to suicide prevention lines and his personal cell phone. Sunny escorts the responders outside as they give her advice. She thanks them and closes the door. Ahmaad looks lost, hopeless and embarrassed sitting on the couch. "Don't feel sorry for me. You can still go. I just didn't know what else to do Sunny. I just don't know what to do." Sunny sits next to Ahmaad.

She grabs his head and lays it down in her lap while Ahmaad cries all of his emotions out. She can't find any words to say so she just cradles Ahmaad and rubs his head until he falls asleep. Sunny gently eases his head off her lap and onto the couch. She puts a blanket over Ahmaad and goes outside to collect herself. She feels under attack and overwhelmed. She doesn't know where to go who to talk to or who to depend on. She feels alone and afraid of what she will do next. "Really God? Are you fucking kidding me? I HATE YOU!" Sunny screams at the top of her lungs in her back yard. Causing her voice to echo through the morning sky. Sunny writes Ahmaad a note, "I'm not far I will be back. Call me." She gets in her car and drives over to Tyra's house. She calls her the entire ride over but Tyra doesn't answer. She sees Dre's truck in her parking lot. "This slut bitch." Sunny says to herself. Without even thinking about it, Sunny goes to the door and waits until someone walks out so she can walk in without being buzzed in.

She bangs on Tyra's door. No answer. She bangs again. "Who the fuck is it?" a man's voice yells out as he snatches the door open. It's Dre standing there shirtless. Sunny rolls her eyes and barges in. "Tyra! Tyra! I need to talk to you." Sunny goes to Tyra's room where she is standing butt naked looking for something to cover up with. "Sunny who the fuck do you think you are to be barging into my shit like this? What the fuck is your problem?" Tyra yells. "Look T, some real fucked up shit is happening and I need my friend. Why the fuck you ignoring me for this trash ass nigga?" Sunny says. "Watch your fucking mouth bitch. He aint trash…that's my man." Tyra says defending her man's honor. "Your man? Tuh…these niggas for everybody I see."

Tyra looks at Sunny after tying her robe. "what the fuck you trying to say Sunny?" Sunny shakes her head, "Nothing. I just…. Never mind. Gone about your business." Sunny walks out the door. Tyra grabs Sunny's arm and pulls her back. "No bitch you came over here, barging in, blowing my phone up so what's up? What you get yourself into now?" Tyra asks. Sunny is hurt by Tyra's reaction. "I'm not saying shit while this nigga is here. So whenever you get some time maybe you can pencil me in. Other than that I will figure my shit out on my own. Take care." Sunny says while pulling away from Tyra's grip. "Hold up. Wait a got damn minute. You don't get to do this. You don't get to come up in my shit causing all this confusion and not tell me what the fuck is going on! Sit your ass down and start talking got damnit!" Tyra yells out in frustration. "Aye T I'll holla at you later." Dre says. "Dre you don't have to go nowhere just chill." Tyra says. "Naw I'm smooth. Handle whatever going on with your girl. I'll be through later on." Dre says as he walks down the hallway and out the door. "Now you fucked up my dick action and made my man leave. I haven't spoken to you since like a month ago and now you just pop up with drama. This better be good." Tyra says with her arms crossed and attitude on ten. "Ahmaad hung himself." Sunny says with no emotion and stone eyes. Tyra puts her hand over her mouth. "Sunny. Oh my God. Is he dead?"

Sunny answers, "No. I cut him down in time. I was going to leave him for good and he does this so I would stay. It just happened this morning." Tyra looks at her friend and all the anger and resentment she had for her went out the window. She just wanted to comfort her friend and help her through her troubles. "Sunny, you got to leave him. He's dangerous and he needs help! You gotta get yourself and your baby out of there. Come here and live with me. We will work it out. But you have to leave him." Tyra voices her concern. "T, how can I leave him when he's down like this? He saved my life. I owe him the same." Sunny says while her emotions and feelings start to rush in all at once. "You don't owe him shit! You owe yourself and your baby happiness and love. Fuck his crazy ass! Sunny get out of there, now!" Sunny breaks down. She's so beaten down emotionally she doesn't know what to do or how to fix it. "Help me, T.

Please. Please T, help me. Help me!" Sunny cries out for help. She cries from the pit of her belly. Tyra holds her tight and rocks side to side. "I'm here baby. I got you. Let that shit out. You going to have a damn heart attack if you keep this up! I got you Sunny. I got you baby!" Tyra ushers her friend to her bed and lays her down. "It's okay baby. I got you." Tyra reassures her friend. She goes into the bathroom and gets a washcloth.

She wets it with warm water and washes the tears from Sunny's face. Sunny is moaning out in heart ache. Tyra takes Sunny's clothes off and draws her a bath. She helps Sunny get into the bathtub. Sunny eases down into the hot water. It feels so good against her skin. She slides down under the water so that her eyes and nose are just above the water line. Tyra puts in a Najee jazz CD and lights three candles on the bathroom countertop. She grabs a comb and brush from under her sink. She kneels down against the bathtub and takes the hair clip out of Sunny's hair. Her tresses fall into Tyra's hand as she catches them before hitting the water. She lays Sunny's hair on the edge of the tub and starts to comb her hair from the ends up. "Tyra, you're always taking such good care of me. I don't know what I would do without you T. I need you." Sunny grabs Tyra's hand and kisses it. "I'm not going anywhere Sun. I will always be here for you. Always. Now just relax. You need to ease your mind and body for a spell." Tyra continues to comb Sunny's hair. Untangling any tangles.

Sunny has fallen asleep. Tyra turns on the hot water because the water starts turning cool. Sunny is awakened by the running water. "I'm going to wash you up Sunny before you turn into a prune." Sunny smiles. Tyra gets a fresh washcloth and towel from her linen closet. She wets the washcloth in the tub and squirts Oil of Olay body wash all over it. She starts with Sunny's neck, scrubbing in circles. Working down her shoulders and arms. Under her breast down her navel. She helps Sunny to stand in the tub so she can wash her womanly parts. She scrubs ever so gentle in her sacred places but gets it squeaky clean. She washes down her legs and in between her toes. Sunny feels like a newborn baby or like royalty.

Tyra then unplugs the drain and turns the water on. She detaches the shower head and rinses all of the soap off Sunny. Tyra grabs the towel and wraps Sunny in it while helping her step out of the tub. She helps her back into her room where she dries off every spec of water on Sunny's body. She gets her coconut oil and starts to moisturize Sunny's skin while massaging her from her neck to the bottom of her feet. Sunny is completely relaxed. "Now just lie down for another half hour if you can. Just relax. No noise no words no thoughts… just Najee. Okay?" Tyra lays down beside Sunny. She runs her fingers ever so gently across Sunny's skin. "T, can you make me cum? I really miss you making me cum T." Tyra smiles, "You miss cumming for me Sun? I miss making you cum." Tyra slides down the bed so that her face is in front of Sunny's lady pond. She nuzzles against Sunny's pussy lips with her lips until her lips open up enough to expose the hood of her clit.

Tyra waste no time. She swirls and sucks around Sunny's clit fast and hard until her clit comes out of hiding. Sunny's pussy responds by making smacking noises as her wetness oozes down her pussy lips and kissing the crack of her ass. Tyra slows down her speed and goes directly to the left side of Sunny's clit. The spot that's most sensitive. She licks and sucks and licks the left side of Sunny's clit until it starts percolating on Tyra's tongue. Sunny's moans are guttural, deep. It's as if she's sinking into the bed. All of the walls and floors disappear. Everything is black and smoky with a tiny purple light shining brighter and brighter just above her. The closer she gets to climaxing the brighter the light gets and the warmer her body becomes. Tyra has her right where she wants her. Tyra's takes her Index and middle fingers and buries them inside Sunny's pussy while she sucks her clit.

She strokes in and out. Sunny's pussy welcomes Tyra's fingers as they swallow them whole. Tyra reaches Sunny's G-spot. She felt something fleshy inside Sunny and when her fingers touched it Sunny convulsed. Tyra continued to stroke Sunny's spot with her fingers and her warm wet mouth continuously sucking on her rock hard clit. "Tyra. Tyra baby I'm cumming. I'm muthafucking cumming baby. I'm cuuummmmminnggggg!" Sunny shakes violently and contorts her body. Her pussy contracted so strongly it forced Tyra's fingers out of her pussy. She squirts down Tyra's neck and chest as if her pussy just popped a shaken bottle of Moet. Tyra tries to catch some of Sunny's nut in her mouth like a water fountain. "Yes that's my yummy. Give me some more yummy! I want some more!" Tyra says as cum dribbles out the sides of her mouth.

Sunny pushes Tyra's head away from her crotch. She can't take another lick. Her pussy is ultra-sensitive. "Tyraaaa help me. Fuuuuuck I'm still cumming! Teeeeee!" Sunny's body looks as if she has electrical currents shooting from head to toe. She's having multiple smaller orgasms after she squirted. She's never had an orgasm like this. She knows it's because Tyra, mentally fucked her first and killed the game by ending it with a physical fuck. Tyra trails kisses along Sunny's spine very lightly as Sunny's body starts to calm down and return to earth. "I love my yummy. I love my Sunny even more." Tyra says with all sincerity. Sunny stares into Tyra's eyes while laying on her side in the fetal position, soaking in all the love affection and attention Tyra is giving her that she desperately needs. This is all Sunny wants.

She just wants to be loved and cherished. The only component that's missing is receiving this love from a man not a woman. "I love you too, T. I don't wanna go. You've made me feel fucking incredible. You took all of my burdens and worries away in just an hour. Like, how is that even possible? I promise to try and come back tomorrow. I just really need to spend some time with my friend. Let me get up and check on this man." Tyra doesn't put up a fuss. She knows what's on Sunny's plate and she doesn't want to add anything to it by expressing her jealousy and desire to want her to herself. Tyra simply says, "I hope to see you and my yummy soon." The two giggled and embraced. Sunny hadn't felt this relieved and satisfied in such a long time. "I'll text you, love." Sunny says while walking out the door.

Ahmaad is asleep on the couch when Sunny returns. He looks so peaceful she doesn't want to wake him. She starts unpacking her things and tidying up the house. "I didn't hear you come in." Ahmaad says while standing behind Sunny. "Oh shit. You scared me. You were asleep so I just wanted you to rest you know. How you feeling Maad?" Sunny asks... "To be honest, blessed. Seeing you putting your things back where they belong give me so much joy. I know I need to get myself some help but I'm hoping we can do this together Sun. I promise not to pressure you or guilt you into anything. Going forward I want us to be honest and open with each other. No more secrets Sunny. I swear on my life." Sunny thinks to herself how worthless his promise is, since he can so easily throw his life away. "Okay Ahmaad. One step at a time. First we have to get you some counseling. Me as well and then we can discuss couple's therapy. Is that a plan?" Sunny asks. "Yeah…anything to get myself together and keep my family together." Ahmaad answers. "You have to get back to work Monday and I need to get the baby from mamas. We gotta get back to some sort of normalcy. So I'm going to get Caleb and when I get home I'll start some dinner. How does that sound?" "Like heaven. I'm going to lay back down. I'm just so exhausted." Ahmaad answers. Sunny kisses him on the cheek, grabs her purse and keys and heads out the door. Sunny drives over to her mom's house to pick up Caleb. "Hey ma, where's my baby?" Sunny's mother rolls her eyes and sighs, "He's taking his nap. Sunny what the hell is going on with you?" Sunny looks confused. "What did I do now?" "You done left this baby here for the last damn time. I don't know what you got going on but I'm hearing a lot of bullshit. The last I heard is you went to go see Ezra and you want his family to see my grand baby? Are you out your fucking mind? Over my damn dead body! Now if you want to fuck your life over and be with a nigga who tried to kill you that's on you but you not taking my grandbaby down with your dumb ass! And I mean that shit! Get your shit together! And until you do this baby stays with me! Period point blank."

Sunny looks at her mother with tears welling up in her eyes. "So you just think you can take MY baby? You think you can take care of my baby better than me? You got me messed up mama. You were never there for me! Never! You think I would let you do that to Caleb? Huh? You think I would let you raise my baby so he can end up molested and raped by 8 years old! Then, grow up falling in love with the wrong people because all he wants is to be loved at any cost?! My life is so fucked up because you weren't there for me! I needed you! I needed a mother! All you did was go to work and treat me like I was a burden! My brother is your golden child and I'm just a fucking mistake! You have no idea how hard I'm trying to hold on! And Caleb is the only reason why I haven't blown my fucking brains out yet! Yeah, the same baby you wrote a fucking check to have me kill! So, fuck you! Fuck you and I'm taking my baby!"

Sunny storms down the hall where she is met by her stepfather. "Sunny, you gotta calm down baby. You not taking this boy out of here and you not going nowhere cuz I got you. I got you Sunny." Sunny's step father embraces her tight and refuses to let go as she tries to free herself from his hold. "Let me go

Pops! Let me gooooo!!" Sunny gives up. She collapses in her step father's arms. "I got you baby, I got you. Don't you worry about another thing ya hear" Sunny is sobbing uncontrollably. Sunny's mother is standing in the hallway with her hands over her mouth and tears streaming down her cheeks. Sunny's stepdad walks her over to the couch and sits down with her while she cries on his shoulder. "You aint got to say nothing else. It's gonna be alright." Sunny's stepdad says. Sunny stops crying. She feels embarrassed but relieved to get some things off her chest that she's always wanted to say to her mother. "I'm.... I apologize for being disrespectful. It's just a lot going on. Maybe it is a good idea for Caleb to stay a while. Ahmaad tried to kill himself this morning." Sunny tells her parents everything that's happened between she and Ahmaad except the abuse and rape he committed against her. "Gal you need to just bring yo butt back home. Just come on back home and get yourself together." Sunny's stepfather advises. "John, she can't just leave that man like that. She got to learn how to work things out now. He been good to her and that baby." Sunny mom retorts. Sunny just rolls her eyes at her mother's comments. "Linda, shut the hell up. Fuck that nigga, he aint did shit but cause this girl stress. Look at her! Listen Su su, you figure it out and decide for yourself. You know you can always come on home. Now I ain't gone pressure you none but now you know."

Sunny felt as if things were starting to turn the corner. She finally was getting the support she desperately needs from her family. She no longer felt alone. After hugging it out with her mom and eating dinner with them and spending time with Caleb, Sunny decides to head back home.

The following weeks Sunny and Ahmaad try to

salvage their relationship by going to couples counseling and Ahmaad goes to a psychiatrist on his own. Sunny has yet to fulfill her end of the bargain by seeking a personal therapist. It's just not important to her and she's busy with working at her first job at Home Depot as a cashier and also taking a full time school load at Wayne State University.

She's working really hard to get herself together so she can get Caleb back. Ahmaad is on the same journey as far as work and school. He's busy with a 20 credit hour load this semester and working fulltime as the county clerk downtown. The two hardly see each other outside of sleeping and their therapy sessions.

It's been six weeks since Sunny has seen Tyra, Calvin or Dre. All three have called and sent text messages but Sunny only responds to Tyra. Tyra seemed to understand why she hasn't' seen Sunny, although she disagrees with her decision to stay with Ahmaad.

"Baby, tomorrow morning we're leaving for Vegas. Just for the weekend." Ahmaad tells Sunny. "Vegas? Huh? What do you mean? Like we're really going to Vegas Vegas?" Sunny asks. "Yes. I wanted to surprise you. We need this. You need this. So pack your bag. We're only staying until Monday. Just in time for school and work."

Sunny jumps out of the bed and leaps into Ahmaad's arms. She kisses him all over his face. "thank you baby thank you mwah! I'm so excited to get the hell outta here! We need this break. I can't believe you!" Ahmaad is delighted. Seeing Sunny happy makes him happy. "You deserve it baby. Now pack up and get some rest because we partying when we touch down nonstop." Sunny rushes over to the closet and starts packing. He didn't have to tell her twice.

The couple touched down in Las Vegas Nevada looking like two kids in a toy store. Eyes big and bright. Mouths wide open, pointing while oohs and ahhs are the only sounds they could articulate. Sunny arrived at their hotel, The Luxor. They stood in awe at the Great sphinx statue with the beautiful black glass pyramid behind it. "We're staying here? In this hotel? Holy fuck babe! This is fucking incredible!" Sunny says while showing all thirty-two of her teeth. "I know right! I can't wait to see our room. Let's go check in!" They couple should wear T-shirts that read "tourists" because they were completely fanning for the glitz and lights of Vegas. The hotel theme of Egyptian royalty was in every detail of the hotel. To the hieroglyphics on the walls, the sphinx statues, the Egyptian sheets and drapery. It was truly something to see. Ahmaad opened the door to their suite slowly.

He peaked his head in and shut the door. “Bae, this shit is out cold son.” Ahmaad said. Sunny pushes him out the way, “Lemme in! Come on!” Sunny pushed the door open and it was as If they just walked through the gates of heaven. The panoramic windows with the view of the city was breathtaking. The giant king size bed, the Jacuzzi and glass showers.

The wet bar and the controller to open the curtains electronically. They were truly in awe. Sunny runs around the room like a little girl laughing in delight. Ahmaad couldn’t take his eyes off her. He hasn’t seen Sunny like this since before she was shot. It was refreshing. He missed seeing his woman happy. “Sunny baby come here.” Ahmaad grabs Sunny’s hand and turns her to face the view of the strip out of the panoramic window. His arms are wrapped around her chest and neck. He’s bending down so that his mouth is close to her ear. "I love seeing you like this. Happy…I vow to do my best to make you feel like this every day of our lives. I just want to see you happy. See you smile. Thank you for coming on this trip with me." Sunny is touched. She caresses Ahmaad's face and pulls him in to her lips. "Thank you. Thank you for trying. Thank you for loving me." Sunny kisses him. "Alright, alright enough of this mushy shit. Let's go have some fun!" Ahmaad says as he smacks Sunny on her ass.

The pair did everything they could possibly think of doing within a 3-day weekend in Vegas. Their hands weren't ever without a tall cup of margarita whenever they were on the strip. They went zip lining, bungee jumping, showgirls, shopping, gambling you name it they did it. Their final night Ahmaad wanted to do something special. He made reservations at Alize restaurant. He bought Sunny a flowy backless white maxi dress with all the accessories he wanted to see on his woman. He laid the dress and accessories on the bed. A note was next to the dress that read, "Meet me at Alize restaurant in 1 hour. There will be a driver in front waiting for you." Sunny put herself together as fast as she could. She's never been more excited.

She curled the last strand of hair and gave herself one last look over before heading downstairs. "Damn I look good tonight. He did good." Sunny says while admiring her figure in the full length mirror. The maxi dress was very seductive and alluring. Her entire back was out with lace adorning her bosom and waistline. A hip length slit was on the right side of the dress which exposed her leg when she stepped forward. The evil eye tattooed on her thigh pierced through with every step Sunny took. Her strappy cork shade Steve Madden heels added the perfect touch, elongating her legs. Sunny looked absolutely intoxicating. The town car driver held a sign up that read her name. Sunny was tickled. She felt like a celebrity. She arrived at the restaurant and the ambiance was breathtaking. She's never been to such a classy upscale restaurant before. Sunny looks around for Ahmaad but can't spot him. Ahmaad is watching her from the back of the restaurant. He can't seem to move. He's never seen her look so beautiful. So angelic.

His dick started to bulge through his linen pants. He adjusted himself and walked towards Sunny. She finally sees him and they both smile. "Damn…you look exquisite. Wow." Ahmaad says while looking at every inch of Sunny. Sunny blushes and coyly says "Thank you." Ahmaad takes her hand and leads her back to their table. "I've taken the liberty of ordering for you already. I hope that's okay?" Ahmaad asks.

“You know I love when you order for me, Ahmaad.” Sunny says while taking a sip of white wine Ahmaad had waiting for her. Ahmaad can’t keep his eyes nor hands off Sunny. He's mesmerized by her enchantment. They talk and laugh over dinner. Talked about all the things they want to do when they come back to Vegas that they didn’t get a chance to do.

8

Sunny's definitely feeling the effects of the wine. She keeps shifting in her seat. Trying not to give way to the fact that her pussy keeps pulsating. Ahmaad has fucked her mind the entire evening. They haven't had sex since he violated Sunny. And now, she's ready. She caught herself biting her lip as he walked to the bathroom. His white linen shirt hugging his muscles on his arms and back. His top button is unbutton exposing the definition in his chest. His two carat earrings are twinkling along with his pearly white teeth. His goatee is lined to perfection. He's letting his hair grow out a bit and it's starting to curl up. Giving an s-curl look but it's all natural. Walking back to their table Sunny notices his dick is hard. He can't hide that 9-inch steel pipe in those linen pants. Sunny gulped down another glass of wine in hopes of calming her pussy down. "So baby where to next?" Sunny asks through squinty eyes. "Marry me. Let's just do it. Let's go to one of these cheesy ass chapels and let's do the damn thing. Marry me Sunny?" Ahmaad says with all seriousness. Sunny laughs.

"Boy stop it. No seriously where we going baby?" Ahmaad grabs Sunny's left hand as he stands up from the table. He gets closer to her and bends on one knee. Marry me, Sunny. I love you, I need you, I don't want to go on another day with you being Mrs. Ahmaad Johnson. Marry me baby?" Ahmaad asks for the last time as he takes out a ring box. Sunny's eyes are bucking. People in the restaurant are staring. "Ahmaad what the fuck? Oh my God. Ahmaad!" Sunny says through gritted teeth. "Marry me Sunny." Ahmaad asks again. Sunny looks into Ahmaad's eyes for what seemed to be an eternity. She was looking for his soul, his heart. She found it. This man loved her like no other man could.

Even though he had his demons, Sunny knew he would take care of her and Caleb the way Ezra couldn't. "Yes. Yes, Ahmaad. I'll marry you. YES!" Before you knew it Ahmaad jumped up and picked Sunny up lifting her off her feet. They kissed passionately as a single tear fell from Ahmaad's eye. The patrons in the restaurant were oohing and ahhing and some even clapped. Sunny cheeks were turning red. "Let's go get married." Ahmaad says. He reaches in his wallet and leaves $300 on the table to cover the bill. The couple get into the town car together and the driver takes them to Chapel of the Flowers on Las Vegas boulevard. "Holy shit Ahmaad. You're fucking crazy. Are we really doing this?" Sunny asks as they pull into the parking lot of the chapel. Beautiful flowers were all over the establishment. So many flowers that it could've been mistaken for a botanical garden. "Yes I'm fucking crazy for you. I really want you as my wife but you have to want me as your husband too for this thang to work. You got cold feet already girl?"

Ahmaad asks while flashing that million-dollar smile. "Let's do it!" Sunny says while squealing like a school girl. The driver opens the door for the couple and they go inside to speak to the officiant. They signed a marriage license, handed over their ID's and before you know it you heard, "You may now kiss your bride." From the officiant. Ahmaad grabbed the Sunny's face with both hands and kissed her as her husband for the first time. Sunny felt as if she were in a dream. She felt so carefree and open to anything. It's as if she were watching a movie not realizing she is the star. "Baby I'm Mrs. Sunny Johnson? Like, I'm your wife?" Sunny asks after kissing her husband. "Your my wife and I'm your husband. This is the happiest day of my life Sun." The two newlywed's kiss again and walk back to the town car where the driver congratulates them and takes them back to the hotel.

Their flight leaves in less than eight hours. "Wait! You're supposed to carry me over the threshold like in the movies and shit babe." Sunny says to Ahmaad as he sticks the keycard in the door of their hotel room. "Come here wife!" Ahmaad scoops Sunny up as if she weighed 20 pounds. Sunny giggles in delight. Ahmaad tosses her in the bed causing her hair to cover her face while she squeals and laughs. Ahmaad lays beside her and moves her hair from her face ever so gently. "Sunny, I want to talk to you seriously. I hurt you. I raped you, Sunny. I will never forgive myself for taking advantage of you the way I did. You need to hear me say what I did out loud. I am ashamed and humiliated by my actions. But more than anything I am remorseful. I would rather die before I ever hurt you like that again. Please forgive me Sunny." Sunny's bottom lip starts to quiver. Ahmaad's tears are staining his cheeks.

She sees how difficult and necessary it was for him to say these words to her. She can't help but to forgive Ahmaad and welcome him back into her life her heart and her pussy. "I forgive you Ahmaad. I forgive you. Kiss me." Ahmaad climbs on top of Sunny and kisses her deeply. Nibbling on her bottom and upper lips. Tasting the wine and strawberries from her mouth as their tongues dance together in harmony. Ahmaad hands find Sunny's breast. He squeezes her breast with hand causing her nipples to protrude. Ahmaad feels her hard nipples piercing through the lace of her dress. He pinches and twist Sunny's nipples. Making them more erect and causing her wetness to flow. Sunny takes her arms out of the dress, exposing her bare breasts. Ahmaad didn't waste any time devouring them as if he were a starving animal in heat. He swirls his tongue around her nipples as if they were popsicles.

Ahmaad's hand traveled down Sunny's stomach and into her thong panty. "Damn baby. You're soaked. You know what this does to me. Put my face in it wife." Ahmaad commands. Sunny slips her dress off leaving her soaking wet thongs on and buries Ahmaad's face in her crotch. Ahmaad growls and moans. He bites on her pussy lips through her panties. Gently, not hard. He rubs his entire face on the crotch of her wet panties. He takes the crotch of the panty and sucks the pussy juice off. Sunny is so turned on. She loves watching him in his primal state. "God I love your pussy. I love the way it smells the way it tastes the way it looks and feels on my face and on my dick. I love the way your clit responds to my touch and dances on my tongue. I love my wife's pussy." Sunny looks down at Ahmaad and seductively bites her index finger. "Put your wife's clit in your mouth and suck on it until she cums."

Sunny is in charge now. Ahmaad dives in, opening her pussy lips with both hands as if he's opening the bedroom curtains to let the morning Sun brighten the room. He sucks and nibbles as if her clit were a pacifier until it became rock hard and started vibrating. "Ahmaad I want you to suck it but in circles fast got damnit. Do you feel my clit jumping husband? Huh? She ready to cum for her husband." Ahmaad does what he is told. He looks as if he's doing neck rolls in circles with a mouthful of Sunny's pussy. Sunny arches her back, her legs automatically lock and she squirts on her husband's chin. "Fuck fuck fuck fuck!!" Sunny screams. Ahmaad's dick is so hard and his balls are so heavy it hurts. "I need to be inside you baby. Let me in." Ahmaad says while teasing Sunny with the head of his dick against her drenched pussy lips. "Come in husband. Come the fuck in!" Ahmaad slides his steel inside of his wife.

The feeling is unexplainable. His eyes roll back in his head and his throat lets out the deepest moans Sunny's ever heard from him. He can't hold his nut it's leaking out with every stroke. He is trying to hold back but can't. His balls tighten and released all of its tension inside Sunny's walls. "Ahhhhh Fuck! Sunny fuck! You see why I'm fucking crazy over you? Look what you do to me! Turn that ass over." Ahmaad takes his sloppy wet dick out and turns Sunny over on her stomach. Even though he just came his dick is still hard and he has a lot more left in him. "I'm going to make you love me like I love you. I'm going to give you everything your heart desires. You are mine.

Mine baby. You're fucking mine." Ahmaad says in Sunny's ear as he drapes himself over her back and slides his dick back inside her walls. Sunny is in ecstasy.

Ahmaad sits up and watches his dick slide in and out of his wife's pussy. Getting more and more wet while Sunny plays with her clit. "Make your wife squirt again. You know what to do." Ahmaad turns Sunny back over and picks her up, wrapping her legs around his waist. He walks over to the window and slams Sunny's back against it. Sunny winces because the glass is cold on her skin. Ahmaad reaches around and puts his dick back inside Sunny while he balances her against the window with the Las Vegas city lights twinkling as if it were a light show. Sunny feels all 9 inches inside her in this position. She tries to hold on to the window for balance but can't. "I got you. Just take this dick don't worry about nothing else." Ahmaad says in between breaths. Sunny relaxes her arms and leans back even more on the glass while Ahmaad holds her waist and thrust vigorously. He found her g spot.

Sunny's back is sliding on the glass while Ahmaad's dick slides in and out of her pussy, punching on her g spot like a speed bag. "Baby I'm about to cum! Baby help me I'm cumming!!" Sunny screams as she squirts all over Ahmaad's dick. Her cum splashes up onto their stomachs and faces. It was as if he struck oil. Pussy juice was everywhere. Sunny slipped back off the glass window and was in a half back bend. Ahmaad didn't want to fuck up her nut so he had to hold on for dear life while trying to inch towards the chair near the desk. He finally gets to the chair and sits down with his dick still nestled inside of Sunny's hot spring. He trails kisses up and down her neck and breast while she catches her breath. She grabs his chin and shoves her tongue down his throat. She wants to taste everything he has to give her. Sunny starts to ride Ahmaad slowly while kissing him.

Her pussy is so wet, his dick keeps slipping out when she raises up but, when she sits back down it slides right back in just like there was an oil slick along her pussy lips. “Baby you keep bouncing on my dick like that I’m liable to have a seizure. I can’t take it Sunny. Sunny got damn I can’t hold on.” “Give it to me daddy. Give me the rest of my nut.” Sunny says while bouncing down on Ahmaad’s dick harder and harder until she feels it thump inside of her, releasing all of his seeds. Ahmaad wraps his arms around Sunny’s waist and burrows himself inside her bosom while shaking violently. Sunny plants kisses on his sweaty forehead and face. “If we could have babies, this right here would’ve made twins.” The newlyweds laugh together. Ahmaad finally calms his breathing down and picks his wife back up and places her in the bed with his dick still inside her. "I just want to lay inside you all fucking night. You're mine Sunny. You're my wife. I'm the happiest man alive." Ahmaad kisses his wife passionately.

"And I'm the happiest woman alive, But I have to pee baby." "Go head and pee then." Ahmaad says. "you won't let me go baby hehehe" Sunny says while trying to get up but Ahmaad holding her tighter. "I told you I can't let you go. You might as well let it rip." Sunny looks at Ahmaad like he's lost his mind. "Boy I am not peeing on you! You are so nasty!" Ahmaad chuckles "You my got damn wife. We can be as nasty as we want. You mine. Besides I always been curious about that though." "About what? Getting peed on?" Sunny asks in a high pitched voice. Ahmaad cheeks turn red, "Yeah man. I mean I don't know. You making me feel like a weirdo." Ahmaad says while his embarrassment creeps through. "Aww baby don't be turning red on me. You can tell me anything and I won't judge you. But you really want me to pee on you?" Sunny asks. "I asked you didn't I wife?" Ahmaad says.

Sunny looks at her husband, "What am I gonna do with you huh? You just full of surprises" Sunny starts nibbling on Ahmaad's ear. His erogenous spot. She lets pee trickle out and uses her Kegel muscles to control the flow. It's warm and she feels it pooling on his groan. Ahmaad is biting his lip and moaning. Sunny is watching him while still nibbling on his ear and now licking down his neck. She lets her pee flow full blasts and starts sucking on Ahmaad's neck aggressively. Leaving passion marks. Ahmaad dick is fully erected again and he starts thrusting and pumping his dick inside Sunny. "You a nasty muthafucka. That's why I married you, you know that?" Sunny says. Ahmaad grabs Sunny's head and sticks his tongue down her throat while pumping like a jack rabbit. Pee is splashing everywhere with each thrust.

The slapping and smacking noises fill the air. Sunny feels Ahmaad's dick pulsate. She knows he's about to cum again. Ahmaad takes his tongue out of Sunny's mouth and looks her dead in the eyes. He gets lost in her gaze. His breathing is heavy, he doesn't speak. He's in another dimension. "Cum for me baby. Fill me up with your babies. Bust a nut for me husband!" Ahmaad lets go. He breaks his stare and squeezes Sunny waist tight so she couldn't move. His toes curl and legs stiffen. His moans are 3 octaves higher than normal. His body is trembling. Sunny squeezes her pussy walls and Ahmaad squealed like a pubescent thirteen-year-old boy. "No more no more! I can't take no more Sun, fuuuuck!"

Sunny kisses Ahmaad's forehead and slowly lifts up and slides his dick out. He winces and tenses up with every inch that slid out. His dick was hella sensitive. "Baby...you gotta call housekeeping and I'm gonna hide. I don't want them to know I pissed in this bed." Sunny chuckles. "Oh so you just gone leave me with the dirty work. You know we are one now. We in this together Mrs. Johnson. "We are in everything else together except this pissy situation. Hehe I love you babe. I'm about to shower...as a matter of fact why don't you join me." "Now you talking."

Ahmaad and Sunny has been back from Vegas for a week now and she still hasn't told anyone they're married. Ahmaad wanted to tell the world but Sunny convinced him not to. They both wore their rings but never confirmed anything with anybody. The high from the trip is fading and the reality of what Sunny committed herself to is sinking in.

Sunny is in the kitchen washing dishes. Ahmaad comes home from school and sneaks behind her and kisses her on the neck, "How's my wife doing?" Ahmaad says. Sunny jumps. She didn't hear Ahmaad she was daydreaming about everything that's happened within the past week. "Don't scare me like that!" Sunny yells at Ahmaad. "I'm sorry baby I didn't mean to scare you." Sunny rolls her eyes and slams the faucet down to cut off the water. "Yeah well you did. Excuse me." Ahmaad scrunches his face. "Whoa, what the fuck is up with you? Is everything good?" Sunny tries to check herself and hold back from lashing out. "I'm cool Maad. My bad for snapping." Sunny walks to the bedroom to get her clothes on for work. Ahmaad follows her. "I thought you were off today?" Ahmaad asks. "Nope." Sunny is dry and short. "Oookay. Well whatever is bothering you I hope you get over that shit quick."

Ahmaad walks out the room. "Excuse me? I don't have shit to get over nigga. If something was wrong with me I would let you know. I said I'm straight so leave me the fuck alone and stop trying to start an argument. Damn." Ahmaad walks back in the room,

"Yo who the fuck you think you talking to like that? You got me fucked up Sunny. Take your dumb ass to work." Sunny puts on her airmax 95's, "Gladly muthafucka." She grabs her purse and keys and slams the door behind her. "Why the fuck did that just happen? What is wrong with me, damnit!" Sunny says talks to herself. She pulls into Home Depot and sits in her car to clear her head. She grabs the half pint of Hennessy in her glove box that she purchased this morning and drunk half. She sprays her breath with Binaca, checks her lipstick and hair and heads into work to punch in. It's been four hours since the start of her shift and she's daydreamed for most of it.

Thinking of Tyra. Missing Ezra. Longing for her baby. "Today just aint my day I guess." Sunny thinks to herself. "Well well well, if it isn't Miss love em and leave em."

Sunny spins around to see who said that…."Calvin? Oh my goodness, Hi. How are you?" Sunny asks nervously. "I'm cool. So you work here I see. That's what's up. You know I called you for a few weeks. I even drove past your crib out of concern. I'm glad to see you're doing okay." Calvin says while looking like a centerfold in his police uniform. "That was shitty of me. I apologize. I'm just messy you know. Got a lot going on. And to be honest…. I just didn't know how to communicate that to you so I chose to ignore. Which I'm regretting like a muthafucka right now cuz you're looking pretty hot in that uniform, sir." Sunny is flirting now, trying to break the tension. "You trying to make a blue black nigga blush. Yeah well I ain't fucking with your ass I'm just glad you straight." Calvin says trying to regain control.

The power struggle is real right now. "Oh so you not fucking with me anymore? Ok, I don't blame you. Well Mr. Officer, if there's anything I can assist you with; nuts, screws, hammers and what not, please don't hesitate to ask. I'm just an aisle away. You take care of yourself." Sunny starts walking away. She knows if he calls after her she still has this man by the balls. She feels his eyes on her ass so she switches just a little harder. But still…nothing. He doesn't take the bait. "Damn, I guess I lost my mojo." Sunny says to herself as she starts to restock the shelves of drill bits. "Excuse me Miss, but I got a question about this hammer." Calvin says as he walks down Sunny's aisle. Sunny couldn't hold her smile in. "Ah yes, the hammer time 3000. Excellent choice. It will nail anything with one strike." Sunny responds. "Yeah that's perfect for me because every time I hit I never miss. I mean never."

Calvin says while being more aggressive by walking up on Sunny and less than 4 inches from her face. Sunny clears her throat and stood back. "So, yeah you should definitely make this purchase. You won't regret it." Sunny says. Calvin gets closer. He sniffs her hair long and hard. Sunny's pussy is getting moist. "Call me when you're ready for me Sun Shine. I'll be waiting." Calvin whispers this in Sunny's ear and walks away. If she were an ice cream cone, there would be a spill on aisle 7. "Damn I don't remember him being that fine. Shit. If Ahmaad keep on my nerve that's exactly who I'm calling got damnit." Sunny says to herself as she stocks.

Sunny's shift is over and she walks into the parking lot after punching out to get in her car. Ahmaad is parked next to her playing Beauty by Dru Hill with all of his windows rolled down and his bass and treble all the way up. “Oh my fucking God this nigga is embarrassing!” Sunny looks obviously annoyed as she rolls her eyes at Ahmaad. Ahmaad gets out the car with a dozen red roses.

Sunny can’t help but blush; She loves shit like this. “Oh now you see a nigga got roses for you, you wanna give me a smile huh?” Ahmaad Says while skinning and grinning at the idea of knowing his lady well. “GImme my roses nigga. I deserve these damnit.” Sunny snatches the roses out of Ahmaad’s hand and smells them. She can’t help but keep a permanent smile on her face. “I’m sorry. For whatever I did. See you at home.” Ahmaad kisses Sunny on the cheek, gets in his car a pulls off. Sunny’s coworkers were all in being nosey watching from their cars. Sunny puts the flowers in the back seat and she looks up as she closes the back door on her escort and peeps Calvin's car at the very end of the parking lot. "What the fuck?" Sunny says to herself. She gets in the car and pulls out fast to get to Calvin's car. As she approaches he flicked his lights on.

Sunny didn't stop she pulled alongside him. His head was down and he looked like his hand was just caught in the cookie jar. He rolled down his window. "What the fuck Calvin?" Sunny asks him. "Get in the car for a minute, okay?" Calvin asks but Sunny is hesitant. She doesn't know if she should run off or chop it up with him. Sunny shuts off her car and gets inside Calvin's. "So, what? you about to chloroform me now? What the fuck is up Calvin? You stalking me for what? I shouldn't even be in your car! you got me feeling a way."

"I know I do but listen Sunny. You may not like me after I tell you what I have to tell you. But I'm keeping it real with you because I'm really fond of you. But your boyfriend: excuse me, now husband... Hired me to follow you around and catch you in some bullshit. He thought you were cheating so he hired me as a P.I. I'm so fucking sorry yo." *SLAP* Sunny slaps Calvin.

"How fucking dare you! Don't you ever call me again!" Sunny tries to get out of the car but Calvin is holding her by her arm. "Wait, wait Sunny! Just please give me a chance to explain myself." Sunny snatches her arm away. "This should be good. I'm listening." Sunny crosses her arms and rolls her eyes. "One of my buddies hit me up asking if I could look out for one of his homeboys at the 34th district court. Said he was the county clerk and his girl been doing him dirty. I do P.I. work on the side so I agreed. I met your boyfriend and he told me y'all story. Said he knew you were doing something he just didn't know with who. I've been following you for about two months now and to be honest, I wasn't expecting you to be who you are and I got caught up. I really like you Sunny and that is the only reason why I'm risking my job and telling you everything." Sunny's leg is shaking. "So what did you see? What did you tell him?" Sunny asks. Well I have pictures of you going to Tyra's house, pictures of you going to Dre's house and that's it. I told him about Tyra and you going to see your sons Father. That's all I have on you. Here's your file." Calvin gives Sunny her file and there's a dozen pictures of her going into Tyra and Dre's apartment and even a snap of her going inside the prison to visit Ezra. "So what do you want me to do with this information? Why are you telling me? So you can get some pussy?" Sunny asks. "To be honest with you, no. I think you should seriously start thinking about plans on leaving this nigga. He aint wrapped too tight. Believe me. And when he found out you went to see Ezra he tore up my entire office. He's still paying off the damages. I just couldn't keep this shit from you because I like you too much." "He's my fucking Husband Calvin. Did you know we eloped a week ago? We fucking eloped! I just can't believe this shit yo. Like, every time I want to move forward with this nigga some fuck shit pops up. I just want to be fucking happy. Why is that impossible for me?" Sunny starts crying. Calvin grabs her hand in hopes of comforting her. Sunny snatches her hand away. "Don't ever touch me. You're no better than him." Sunny gets out of the car and slams the door. Calvin pulls off. Sunny sits in her car a while to gather her thoughts and think of her next move. "Okay, he wants to hire P.I.'s. I'm always running the streets doing my own thing, it's time I watched his ass for once." Sunny grabs her phone out of her purse and calls

Calvin. "So what else aren't you telling me, Calvin. What else do you know? You might as well tell me." There's a 5 second pause, "He has a baby Sunny. With some woman named Veronica. He also wanted me to serve her with DNA test orders. And he received the results back before you two went to Vegas."

Sunny's heart drops. "That's really his kid? Wow." Sunny says. "Listen Sunny I understand my role in this but I never wanted to hurt you. This has never happened to me. I handled you wrong and I'm sorry. But everything I've ever expressed to you about how I feel for you and the beautiful person I know you are is real. I meant all those things. You can call me anytime." Calvin says. "I appreciate your candor. Just give me a minute to figure shit out. Take care Calvin. I'll be in touch." Sunny ends the call. Sunny is battling between telling Ahmaad everything and keeping it to herself until she thinks of a plan. "I need to smoke, fuck this shit." Sunny calls Dre. "Aye what up can I get a bag? Ok cool you delivering? Bet meet me at the dust. I'll be at the bar."

Sunny drives to the Stardust lounge in Inkster to get a much needed drink and their famous smothered pork chop dinner. Sunny goes inside stardust and places her order with the owner of the lounge, Ms. Pat. Ms. Pat greets everyone by name and with a warm smile. She makes you feel like you're at home. "What can I get you baby?" Ms. Pat asks. "Lemme get a smothered pork chop dinner Ms. Pat. and how you doing today by the way?" Sunny asks. Ms. Pat flashes that million-dollar smile, "Oh baby I'm blessed, you know Ms. Pat aint gonna complain. The real question is how are you doing, baby? How you been making out since everything? Every time I see you I just smile because you are a living miracle." Ms. Pat has a way with words; making Sunny feel comforted and at home. "You right Ms. Pat. I really am a miracle. God didn't have to spare me but for whatever reason He did. I don't know why, but He did." Sunny replies. "He did because he aint through with you yet. You're supposed to be here and don't forget that. God has plans for you and don't let anybody get in the way of your happiness and your destiny, you hear? I see so many of y'all youngsters that don't take advantage of your second chances. But you Sunny, you take it and run and don't you dare stop." Ms. Pat grabs Sunny's hand and squeezes it tight, reassuring her that everything will be alright. Sunny couldn't help but get emotional. She held back her tears and just nodded her head. "Now lemme make the best smothered pork chops you done ever had. Give me 20 minutes' baby." Sunny nods, "Yes ma'am. Thank you Ms. Pat. Thank you." Ms. Pat taps Sunny's hand, gives her wink and holds her head up high as she walks back to the kitchen to put her foot in Sunny's dinner.

Sunny orders a Hennessy and coke while she waits for Dre and her food. "Sup stranger." Dre whispers in Sunny's ear startling her. "Nigga, that's how fools get popped." Sunny says sarcastically. "Run up then. Aye I'm happy as hell you asked me to meet you here. I'm hungry then a muthafucka." Dre says while rubbing his belly. "I know right, I just ordered me a dinner. Lemme see that bag though." Sunny says. "Damn stall me out D-Bo. I got you but not in here. What you drinking on? You look like you need a friend. Allow me to be your friend. Come and talk to daddy." Dre says flashing his gold plated grill. Sunny rolls her eyes and sighs, "Hen and coke nigga." "Excuse me, bring three more of these over. One for you two for me. Cool?" Dre asks. "I guess."

Sunny says snarky. "So what's going on with your fine ass? Why you look so damn stressed? You too cute to be frowned up and shit. What that nigga aint doing?"

Sunny looks at Dre through her squinted eyes, "Why you fucking my girl Tyra? She not even your type so what's up with you and her?" Sunny asks with as much attitude as she could conjure. Dre smirks, "Man she cool people you know. And she got a fat ass and I'm a man. You see that ass and you know what her mouth do. Not to put you on blast but you know what's up. We just having fun. Why you asking anyway? I should be asking you the same thing. She aint your type so why you fucking her? You leading that girl on and you know it. All she does is talk about your big head ass. So what's up with that?" Dre asks after slamming his first Henny and coke back. Sunny is irritated. "Ok this was a bad idea. I just need my weed. We can stop talking now." Dre chuckles, "Damn you on tip. Ok I'm being an asshole I apologize. My bad shorty. Ok? Here this bag on me for being a jerk."

Sunny relaxes a bit. "Ok that's more like it. And thank you. And to answer your question I Love Tyra. But I'm not leaving my man for a bitch. Not never. So you know, it is what it is. Just don't fuck her over. She is too good of a person for that. That's all I'm saying." Dre nods his head, "Fa sho. Respect." Ms. Pat brings out both dinners and cashes Sunny and Dre out. "Follow me to my car." Dre tells Sunny. Sunny gets into the passenger seat of Dre's Durango. "You look like you need an eighth to the head. Here you go. That's my let's be friends gift." Sunny takes the bag and examines it. "Ok it looks decent too. I was about to say you must be giving this to me for free because it's some bullshit. Alright let's be friends now. Thanks for the bud, imma get on my way."

Sunny gets out of the truck and gets in her car. She rolls a fat blunt and takes it to the head on her drive home.

9

Ahmaad is playing his video game when Sunny walks through the door. “Hey baby. I was beginning to think you weren’t coming home.” Ahmaad says. “I bet. Naw, I just wanted to get some pork chops from the dust.” Sunny says. “Oh you didn’t think to grab me a dinner huh? Dang you cold. Lemme get a bite of them chops.” Sunny puts her dinner on the dining room table. Ahmaad doesn’t take his eyes off of his game. Sunny completely undresses in the dining room. Strips everything. Even taking her earrings out. “You can get a bite of this pussy.” Sunny says while staring at Ahmaad butt assed naked. Ahmaad looks over at Sunny, looks back at the game. Then it registers that she's naked and he looks back at Sunny and drops his controller. Sunny walks over to Ahmaad on the couch and pulls him up to his feet. "Lay on the floor." Sunny demands. Ahmaad lays down on the floor. Refusing to break eye contact. "You're high as fuck baby." Ahmaad says. "I'm horny as fuck, too." Sunny says while pushing Ahmaad on the ground because he wasn't moving fast enough for her. She straddles his face and opens her pussy lips with her fingers exposing her clit. "Make me squirt on your face. I want you to eat 'ahhh' the fuck 'mmmm' out my pussy." Sunny says, trying to get her demands out while Ahmaad laps up her pussy the moment she straddled his face. "Suck it. Suck my clit. Yeah that's right. Harder. Harder got damnit!" Sunny slaps Ahmaad on the top of his head demanding him to do as she says. Ahmaad furrows his eyebrows, but he does what he's told. His cheeks are drawn in as he sucks Sunny's clit like a Rally's banana shake through a tiny straw. "Now lick it. Yes! Yes, keep licking! Lick it side to side now. Unnnnn Yesssss! Just like that! I'm going to cum so fucking hard Ahmaad. I'm going to nut all over your face. You want me to cum in your mouth don't you? Don't you?"

Ahmaad moans and mumbles "yes" with a mouthful of Sunny. Sunny starts to wobble and lose her balance. Ahmaad holds her up by grabbing her thighs to stabilize her balance. "You know just what to do. That's right don't let me fucking fall. You feel my clit? Huh? Ahmaad, I'm cumming. I'm fucking cumming. Open up your mouth. I want to see my cum. Oh fuck. Open up baaaaabeeeeeee!" Sunny puts her hands in front of Ahmaad's head on the floor for balance. She lifts her bottom up enough to see her ejaculate shoot into Ahmaad's mouth as if her pussy was a water fountain. Sunny collapses onto

Ahmaad's face. The orgasm was too intense for her to remain upright. Ahmaad drank as much of Sunny as he could while never once stopping his tongue strokes on her clit. He couldn't get enough of making Sunny nut.

"Give me all that shit. I know you got some more left for me. Fuck yeah, squirt in my fucking mouth. Mmmm Mmmm" Ahmaad moans. Sunny lifts herself up and slides down his chest as they're now face to face. Sunny takes her hand and rubs her juices in, all over his face. She's trying to catch her breath while her body is convulsing. "You're a nasty lil boy aren't you." Sunny says while Ahmaad sucks and licks on her fingers and hand. Sunny is getting off on this power trip. Sunny takes her middle and ring fingers and stick it inside Ahmaad's mouth. Moving them in a back and forth motion. Ahmaad is here for it. He's sucking everything and anything his tongue will find on her hands. Sunny slides her pointer finger, a third finger, in his mouth; causing Ahmaad to gag. "Baby chill out, hold on hold on." Ahmaad says as he grabs Sunny's wrist and removing her fingers from his mouth. *SLAP* Sunny takes her left hand and slaps Ahmaad across his face with all of her strength. "What the fuck you do that for? Sunny, get up!" Ahmaad demands. He's angry and confused. Sunny snatches her wrist from his grip and spits in his face. "Fuck me you piece of shit!" Ahmaad chokes Sunny with his right hand.

He squeezes until a vein pops out in the middle of her forehead. He lifts her body off of his while choking her and pushes her onto the couch. Sunny struggles to find her breath. She stumbles to her feet. "You never knew how to fuck me right." Sunny says as she stands face to face to Ahmaad with her saliva and pussy nectar covering his face. Ahmaad remains silent. His eyes turn dark. Almost black. His body tenses up. He seems taller. Bigger. Scary. He wipes his face with his hand and grabs Sunny by her neck again. Sunny doesn't fight. He slams her into the wall, never releasing his grip around her neck. He forcefully grabs her leg and wraps it around his waist. He takes his hand off her neck and grabs his shaft.

Forcefully, he enters Sunny. Sunny yelps. "Don't you say a fucking word bitch. Take this dick. This is what you wanted you take it got damnit." Sunny is in a trance. She stares into Ahmaad's dark demented eyes. And she sees the monster, again. This time she isn't afraid. Sunny welcomes the monster. She wants the beast. She wraps her other leg around his waist. Ahmaad takes a couple steps back, causing Sunny to lean against the wall at an angle. He thrust his pelvis forward, violently opening Sunny's life-force. He thrusts again. And again. Causing the drywall to crack behind his force. He walks over to the couch while Sunny bounces on his dick. He grabs her waist and lifts her up. He throws her over the arm of the couch and enters her from behind forcefully. He grabs her face and turns her towards him as far as her neck would allow.

Ahmaad rams his tongue down her throat. “Open your fucking mouth.” Ahmaad yells. Sunny obeys. Ahmaad moves his jaws around to produce saliva and spits directly into Sunny’s mouth. “You want to spit on niggas right? Take that bitch!” Ahmaad forcefully pushes Sunny’s face away from him. He grabs her waist, toots her ass up and forcefully fucks her until he orgasms 45 seconds later. He steps back as his dick slides out of Sunny’s semen filled pussy. He stumbles into the dining room chair. He tries to slow his breathing down and keep eye contact with Sunny. His eyes lighten, his chest and back shrink. He shifts back into his "normal" self. Sunny never looks away. She watches him intently as he transforms before her eyes. "You're really a psychopath." Sunny says abruptly and goes into the bathroom to shower.

As the hot water beats against Sunny's flesh, she's thinking of a masterplan to finally get away from Ahmaad and blow up everything in his world. Ahmaad comes into the bathroom and rips the shower curtains off the rod. "You have the nerve to call me a psychopath? You push and you push and you push until you bring out the worst inside me. You want me to be this monster. You want me to hurt you when all I wanted to do was love you. I see your games, and before you fuck up my life any further, pack your shit tonight and get the fuck out! I'm warning you now, if you stay; somebody will get hurt. You can't fuck with a nigga like me the way you're fuckin with me and get away with it. You have no idea what I've been through. You have no idea of who I really am and what I'm capable of when muthafuckas push me too far. Just leave Sunny! Get the fuck out of my life! What kind of wife are you?"

Ahmaad eyes are blood shot read. His entire body is trembling. He's yelling at the top of his lungs. Veins are popping out of his neck and temples. His face is soaked with tears. He's filled with so many emotions but the one at the forefront is fear and heartache. Sunny is petrified but she also feels sorry for him. She wants to fix him. She isn't thinking about the baby he's hiding, how he hired a private detective to spy on her every move, the rape, the abuse. She can't help herself. She's addicted to feeling needed and wanted despite being in the unhealthiest circumstances. Sunny is standing in the shower, shivering with her arms wrapped around her body. She's too afraid to speak. She's too afraid to keep eye contact for longer than a couple seconds with Ahmaad. Tears escape her eyes and fall down her cheeks. "You're killin me Sunny. You're killin me. I just want a life with you. I want us to be happy. I don't know what to do anymore. I'm sorry about the shower." And just like that, Ahmaad walks out of the bathroom and closes the door. Sunny is shook and more confused than ever.

After a long sleepless night Sunny knows she can't possibly be with Ahmaad despite her feelings for him. And she knows he's too unstable to have a rational conversation on why Sunny's behaving the way she's behaving. After getting dressed she goes into the living room where Ahmaad slept. "Maad, you asleep?" "No. I've been up all night." "Oh. Can we talk?" "Honestly Sunny, I'm done talking. I don't have the energy for talking or anything else. If you're leaving ok if you're staying ok. I don't give a fuck either way anymore. I'm tired." Sunny gets in her feelings. She's becoming angrier by the second. "You're tired? Tuh. Ok bet." Sunny goes into the bedroom they once shared and starts packing her clothes. Ahmaad doesn't move.

She takes bags out to her car one by one as Ahmaad watches. She goes back inside and starts packing up Caleb's entire room. "Can you break my baby's bed down? Ahmaad? AHMAAD?" Sunny yells out to Ahmaad but no answer. She walks into the living room and Ahmaad is gone and so is his truck. "That fucking bastard. Oooh! Fuck you muthafucker!" Sunny loads as much as she can in her car. She leaves a note on the door that reads, ***"be back later for our shit".*** Sunny turns the key in the ignition but the car won't start. She tries over and over and over and the car won't turn over. "What the fuck?!" Sunny gets out of the car and slams the door. She's so frustrated she kicked a dent into the driver's side door. Sunny takes the note off of the front door and goes back inside. She's pacing in the hallway. Trying to think of her next move.

"This muthafucka did something to my fucking car. I know he did." She grabs her cell and dials Ahmaad. "Hello?" Ahmaad answers. "What the fuck did you do to my car Ahmaad? And where the fuck are you?" Sunny asks. "Look bro, you're going to learn to respect me one way or the other. Who the fuck are you talking to like that?" "Ahmaad, I'm not fucking playing with you. What did you do to my fucking car? I'm just trying to get the fuck on and let you move on with your life. This aint what a marriage is supposed to be like! Let me fucking go!" "You can go. Leave…but that's my fucking car. I paid for that. So call your mama or whoever to help you. If not, then you need to stay your black ass at home and work on your marriage. We aint dating. You're my fucking wife! Now let that sink in!" *ENDCALL* Ahmaad hung up on Sunny. "Ooooooh!!!! I hate him! I fucking hate him!" Sunny yells and throws her cell phone across the room.

She plops down on the couch feeling defeated. *RING RING* "What?!" Sunny answers her cell. "Damn, well hello to you too." Tyra says. Sunny didn't look at the screen she just answered the phone assuming it was Ahmaad calling back. "Girl, my bad. Oh shit I'm so glad you called. Can you come pick me up? I need to get out of here like now." "Yeah but where is that nigga of yours at?" Sunny rolls her eyes. "I don't know but he aint here so are you coming or nah?" There's a 5 second pause. "Alright I'm on my way but I'm not pulling up to your house you gonna have to meet me at the end of the block. I'm not fucking with your nigga." Tyra explains. 'Alright just hurry please. Ok? Bye."

Tyra gets to Sunny's house in 20 minutes. She calls Sunny and tells her she's at the corner but Sunny is already there waiting. "Damn, you wasn't playing!" Tyra said. "I'm so tired of this nigga. He did something to my car so I can't go anywhere. I hate him Tyra. I fucking hate him." Sunny looks in Tyra's ashtray hoping to find a tail to spark up. "No bitch aint no tails in there but I got some strong at the crib. So what are you going to do Sunny? Is this just a one day get away or what?" "I don't know T but I'm trying to figure it out. So what's up with you? Why'd you call in the first place?" "Damn it's like that? I just can't call my so called friend to say hi since you never do!" Tyra says sarcastically. Sunny just rolls her eyes and says nothing. "Alright I did have some news to share. So, you heard E and Shalisha got married last week?" Sunny's heart sank. "Who told you that?" "Shalisha put the shit on myspace." Sunny is silent. She goes numb. "She posted pictures and everything. I'll go on her page when we get to the crib." "yeah alright." Sunny stared out the window and sunk as low as she could in the passenger seat. She went completely numb. They arrive at Tyra's apartment and Dre is there playing his Sega Genesis. "Sup doe Sunny." "Sup" Sunny says dryly. "Come on let's go in my room so I can show you her page." Tyra says. Tyra closes her bedroom door and logs onto her computer. "So this nigga real comfy. He living here now?" Sunny asks. "Yeah we getting serious. He moved in a few weeks ago." "Oh…ok. Well if you like it I love it." Sunny rolls her eyes. "I do like it and it's not like I can wait on you to make up your mind for the rest of my life. I want kids too. I want a family. So this is my chance." "The fuck you mean, 'wait on me?' You sound ridiculous." "So you want to sit here in my face and act like you don't know how I feel about you? You know what let's not go there. I'm over it. Here…Here's her pictures of her wedding." Tyra says with an attitude as she gets up and walks out of the room leaving Sunny alone to process the fact that Ezra, her sons father, the man she thought she would spend the rest of her life with yet he tried to take her life; married her ex best friend in prison. Shalisha is smiling ear to ear in every pic. She has on a cheap ten dollar off white lacy baby doll dress from Dots. Ezra isn't smiling but he's embracing her tight. His hands on her ass and hips. There's a picture of them kissing after they said I do. "I feel sick" Sunny knocks over the chair and runs to the bathroom. She starts throwing up every emotion she felt into the porcelain toilet. "Sunny? I'm coming in." Tyra says as she barges into the bathroom. "Damn Sun." Tyra says. She goes out to the hallway to get a wash rag.

She turns on the hot water and wets the rag. "Come here baby. I'm so sorry Sun. I didn't know you would be like this or I wouldn't have shown you." Tyra says as she wipes Sunny's face and mouth. "I'm so hurt and tired T. I don't know how much more I can take. It's always some bullshit happening. I can't win. I can't fucking win. My whole life is just pain and misery. My son is the only thing that brought me joy and I can't even get my shit together to raise him. What the fuck did I do to deserve this? I loved him! I loved that nigga! And he tries to kill me then marries my ex best friend? The fuck T? I'm tired!" Sunny is sobbing uncontrollably. Tyra says nothing. She just holds her friend and lets her get everything out. A few minutes elapses and Sunny finally starts to calm down. "Where that strong at though?" Tyra chuckles. Dre got it. Lets roll up baby." Tyra says while helping her friend up. "Lemme get some mouthwash or something shit." "It's under the sink. Get yourself together and come to the living room when you done. I'm about to roll up." Sunny takes a few swigs of mouthwash and wipes her face. She goes into Tyra's room to get her carmex out of her purse. The pictures are still up on the computer. Sunny feels a hot flash come over her body. Beads of sweat pop up on her forehead. She puts her carmex on and sits at the computer. "Im going to kill these muthafuckas." Sunny starts typing an inbox to Shalisha on her Myspace page. "You think this shit is over?" *SEND* "Sunny what are you doing? Did you send that girl a message on my account?! Sunny what the fuck?!" "I mean what the fuck Tyra. What did you think I was gonna do? Nothing? Tuh, I see everybody got me fucked up. I mean all y'all muthafuckas got me twisted." "Aint nobody got you twisted I just don't want to be involved in no bullshit. Damn!" "Well you involved now bitch so what." "Man here. Fire this shit up." Sunny lights the blunt and takes it to the head. Tyra didn't bother to asks her to hit it she just rolled two more blunts.

Sunny went back in the living room with Dre and Tyra. "That weed from the other night was straight Dre, good looking." Sunny says to Dre. He barely looks up from his game. "Oh fa sho." Dre says. Tyra looks at both of them, "What weed?" Tyra says. "I met up with your mans the other day and he gave me a bag." Sunny says. "Met up with him where?" Tyra asks. "Uh, at the dust. Why? Damn bitch you sounding real accusatory." Sunny says. Dre shakes his head and chuckles. "Aye bro, this what you gotta deal with?" Sunny asks Dre. "Man, you don't know the half. Or maybe you do, shiiiit." Dre says as the two share a laugh. Tyra is pissed. "So y'all gone talk about me like I'm not even here? I mean I don't hear from you in weeks and here it is you met up with my nigga. And what the fuck is that ring on your finger?!" Sunny looks up at the ceiling and takes a long drag of the weed. "We eloped in Vegas." Sunny says. "Sunny. No...No you didn't. Sunny what the fuck?! Oh my God this makes so much sense now! This is why Shalisha and E got married. This must be a message to you or some shit. The fuck is going on Sunny?!" "Who gives a fuck. I need to bust a nut though. Come here T." Dre pauses his game and looks at Sunny. Tyra turns beat red. "Sunny you being disrespectful" "To who? That nigga knows what we do. Dre am I wrong?" Sunny asks. "I mean nah but I want to watch though." Dre says "See he even wants to watch you make me squirt." *BOOM BOOM BOOM BOOM* Someone is banging on Tyra's front door. "Who the fuck?" Dre says as he reaches for his 9mm on the ottoman. Dre goes to the door and looks thru the peep hole. 'Aye some nigga at the door. Who the fuck is this cat Tyra?" "Shit, I don't know. Let me see." "Nah sit your ass the fuck down." Dre snatches open the door, "Aye nigga why the fuck you banging on my shit like you got a fucking problem?" Ahmaad looks around and sees Sunny. "Really? This what you do? You come here? Let's go Sunny. Now!" Ahmaad says. Tyra is scared shitless.

She's frozen on the couch with bugged eyes and mouth open. Sunny continues to smoke her blunt. "You're not my daddy. I don't jump when you say jump." Sunny says "No you're my wife and I'm your husband. Now let's go home and work this shit out. You don't have no business here. Every time some shit go wrong you come here. We not doing this anymore. Let's deal with our shit in the privacy of our home. Now I'm asking my wife to come home." "Alright, I'll be there Maad. I just need a minute." "Sunny, I'm not leaving here without you. You think

I'm gonna leave you here so this bitch can eat your pussy and this nigga wait his turn? I know what time it is. You think I don't know what the fuck it is you do Sunny? Huh? You're my wife. I know everything about you. Now let's go." "Aye Sunny, either you go or stay but I'm not about to let this nigga disrespect my girl in our shit another second. So this can go left really quick."

Dre says with his hand on his glock resting by his side. "Really quick" Ahmaad says as he flashes his .50 Cal Desert Eagle on his hip. "Okay!! Got damnit okay! Let's go Ahmaad." Sunny gets up grabs her jacket and purse and heads out of the apartment with Ahmaad on her heels. "The fuck type shit you on? You think I wouldn't find you? Huh?" "I'm sure you would with the help of your private investigator." Ahmaad stops dead in his tracks. "Yeah, let's go home nigga. Let's settle this shit once and for all."

Sunny yells in the parking lot. Ahmaad unlocks his truck with his keypad and they both get in. “Cat got your tongue?” Sunny says. “Sunny let’s just get home.” The two remain silent on the ride home. Sunny notices all of her belongings weren’t inside her car. She rolls her eyes.

Sunny unlocks the door and heads straight to the kitchen to pour a glass of Hennessy. “That’s part of the damn problem. You always high or drunk. You need to lay off that shit.” Ahmaad says. “That’s funny cause you’re right here with me drinking and smoking. You got your fucking nerve. So what’s good? You got something to tell me? Let’s keep it all the way real. Let’s fucking go.” Sunny says after slamming a double shot and now standing with her arms folded staring Ahmaad down. “Okay yeah I hired a PI. I didn’t trust you, I don’t trust you and you wouldn’t talk to me. So I did what I did.” “Is that it? That’s all you have to say?" "I mean what else can I say?" "You can say a whole fucking lot!" "What can you say? You wanna talk about the fact that you went and seen your baby daddy? You wanna talk about the fact that you getting your pussy ate by your so called best friend every time we get into it? And you meeting up with her nigga going on dates and shit at the dust!! Huh? Your shit stinking like a muhfucka home girl."

"Okay so what! Yes, Tyra eats my pussy. So! I like getting my pussy ate! I'm not fucking a nigga though. I could be fucking all kinds of niggas but I don't! I'm stuck on stupid sticking with your ass! But fuck all that shit muthafucka! You got a fucking baby nigga!! A fucking baby!! And you weren't gonna tell me shit! You taking care of this baby! Going over this bitch house every chance you get playing daddy to her and y'all baby. So you know what? We both living secret lives and we both need to let each other go because if I don't kill you, you're going to kill me because I just don't give a fuck about nothing right now. That's where I'm at with it." Ahmaad is shook. He is speechless. He keeps running his hands through his curly hair. Pacing back and forth and punching the walls.

Sunny sits in the reclining chair and sips another drink while watching Ahmaad punch holes in every wall through the house. "So can you fix my car? I'm not staying here tonight." Ahmaad looks at Sunny with bloody swollen knuckles and sweat dripping down his back. "Alright, Sunny. You win." Ahmaad goes outside and pops the hood of Sunny's car. He fumbles around and closes the hood and starts the car. He walks back in the house, "Just go." Ahmaad says as he walks to their bedroom. "Now you can move your real family in. You don't have to fake like you love my son. You got your own real son now.

Y'all can be one big happy family now. Fuck you for fucking me over! I fucking hate you!" Sunny says while stumbling to her feet. Ahmaad comes back into the living room. "You know something Sunny, I hate me too. I never wanted to hurt you. And I did. You hurt me too. Like no one else ever could or will again. I want us to work out our differences. But I can't keep you hostage. I will always love you. Just go Sun. Just go." Sunny stumbles over to Ahmaad and slaps him across the face causing spit to fly out his mouth. "I hate you!" She slaps him again this time on the other cheek. Ahmaad takes it. His eyes start to water. "I hope you die! I fucking hate you!" Sunny punches Ahmaad in his chest then slaps him. She unleashes blows left and right while screaming 'I hate you' over and over. Her eyes opened the flood gates to her soul. The tears won't stop. Ahmaad takes every blow she delivers until she gets tired and collapses to the ground. Ahmaad picks her up and cradles her like a baby. He takes her in the bedroom and puts her in the bed. She's sobbing uncontrollably, unable to speak. "I love you Sunny. I'm so sorry for hurting you. I'm so sorry my sunshine." Ahmaad refuses to let Sunny go.

He cradles her until she cried herself to sleep. Everything reached a head for Sunny and she had a complete mental break. As soon as Sunny was in a deep sleep, Ahmaad went outside and turned her car off. He came back inside and laid beside Sunny until she woke up 6am the next morning. Sunny felt exhausted and drained. "Let me make you some breakfast baby." Ahmaad says as he kisses her forehead and goes into the kitchen. Sunny doesn't have the energy to fight. She decides to shower and put some clothes on. She wants to see her baby boy after everything that has happened. "I made all your favs baby. Sit down let me fix your plate." Sunny obliges Ahmaad. "I'm going to see Caleb. I just need my baby right now." "Can I see him with you? I miss him Sunny." Ahmaad asks. "No. I want to be alone with him." Ahmaad doesn't say anything. Ahmaad drinks coffee while watching Sunny nibble and pick over her breakfast. She doesn't have much of an appetite. "Before you go. How did you know?" Ahmaad asks. "Asks your PI that you hired. He'll tell you." Sunny says. And she's out the door.

Sunny spends the entire day with Caleb. She takes him to the park and buys him new toys. She felt so much better after connecting with her baby. "Mama I'm coming for my baby. I'm coming for him. I need him mama. I need my baby." Sunny says to Linda. "I know Sunny. I know this was temporary. He's ready for you too. Whenever you're ready. Whatever demons you got Sunny…you gotta let them go. You got to heal your heart baby. Whatever I did or didn't do. Whatever Your father did or didn't do, you got to make peace or it will ruin your life. That son of a bitch who stole your innocence, your sons father trying to kill you…you got to make peace with it all so you can have some quality of life. I'm sorry for failing you baby. Mama is so got damn sorry. I wish I could go back and do things different. I just need you to know that you are my child and I love you. I will always love you and be here. I hope you can forgive me Sunny." "Oh mama. I forgive you. I love you mama." Sunny tells her mom as the two embrace and both shed tears of forgiveness and love. Sunny decides it's time to go back home and talk to Ahmaad. She's had a chance to calm down and really think about the state of their relationship. *RING RING RING* Ezra's sister is calling Sunny. "Hello" "Hey Sunny Ezra's on three-way. "So you get married and I can't? Please don't harass my wife again. You've moved on and so can I. I'm sorry for what I did but leave Shalisha out of this." Ezra says *you have two minutes left* "Are you out of your fucking mind nigga? You know what. You're right. I wish y'all the best. Don't ever call my phone. You, your family, not none of y'all. Stay the fuck out of me and my son's life." Sunny ends the call. *RING RING* "Hey Tyra." "Hey, you straight?"

"Yeah everything is good." Sunny says. "Look Sun, you got me involved in too much bullshit. The price of loving you is too high for me. You got your man on my ass now Shalisha think I betrayed her." Sunny cuts off Tyra "The fuck you mean Shalisha thinks You betrayed HER? The fuck does that mean?" "It means she think I started some bullshit since you inboxed her from my account." Tyra says. "So, you been talking to this bitch? Like, y'all still friends?"

Sunny ask "I mean we cool. We talk." Tyra explains. "How can you be cool with a bitch like her after she did what she did and you claim to love me oh so much? You know what, I don't have time for any of this dumb shit. You, Shalisha and Ezra can go fuck yourselves. I'm done with all of you. Don't ever call me again. Fuck you bitch!" END CALL

Sunny feels like heavy weights have been lifted off her chest. She's able to breathe a little better. She feels vindicated so to speak. She arrives home and sees Ahmaad is still home. She walks in and smells Pine Sol. The smell is making her queasy. "Ahmaad!" Sunny yells. "Yeah bae I'm in the bathroom." "Maad what you do, use the whole gallon of Pine Sol? This shit making me sick to my stomach." "You used to love the smell of Pine Sol. I'm sorry I'll open up the windows. How's my son doing?" Sunny was about to say 'which one' but, she's working on being a better person a better wife and a better communicator. "He's good. I need my baby home. I'm tired of living like this." Ahmaad listens to his wife intently. "I'm here for whatever we need to do Sunny." "What…what happened to your hands Ahmaad? They're bleeding!"

"Oh this? Nah it's nothing…Just spoke to Calvin and got some things straightened out is all. Everything is cool don't sweat it." "You beat the nigga up Ahmaad? He's a fucking cop! What if you go to jail? The fuck Maad?!" "Sunny relax. I know what I'm doing and we're straight. So listen I need you to do me a favor." "Okay what now Maad?" "I need you to take this pregnancy test. You're three weeks late and you're acting like you did with Caleb. Everything is making you nauseous., So I went to CVS and bought you a test. Can you pee?" "Yeah but I'm not pregnant Maad, and how the hell you know I'm three weeks late?" "So you think I don't keep track of your cycles?

You got me fucked up. I know everything about you woman now go take the test. Now that I know I can make babies you know it's a strong possibility."

"Ahmaad I'm not fucking pregnant. And besides we can NOT have another baby right now. I don't even have the first one in my care! What type of shit!"

"Shhh calm down. Baby relax. Sometimes God has a way of making us sit still and submit to His will. So just please take the test and if it's negative we'll get you on some birth control." Sunny snatches the test out of Ahmaad's hand and rolls her eyes as she stomps to the bathroom like a child having a tantrum. She closes the bathroom door and unbuttons her jeans. "I'm not fucking pregnant. This nigga is tripping." She holds the test at an angle to catch her urine stream. Sunny places the cap back on the test and sits it behind the toilet, pulls her pants up, flushes the toilet, washes her hands and walks back out of the bathroom and sits on the couch. "I told you I'm not." "Sunny it hasn't been 3 minutes yet." Ahmaad says as he walks into the bathroom to check the results. Sunny gets up and walks behind him. She sees him smiling in the bathroom mirror. "The fuck is you smiling for?"

Sunny says heavily annoyed. "Because it hasn't been three minutes yet and this shit positive already. Baby we pregnant! Sunny baby! You having my baby!" Ahmaad can hardly contain his excitement. Sunny snatches the test out of his hand. "Lemme see that! Oh my God…no. What? How? Oh my God!" Sunny starts crying. She can't believe she's pregnant at a time like this. "I can't have this baby! What am I going to do with another baby?" "You acting like this baby not mine. Like you got a dead beat baby daddy. Is this my baby Sunny?" Sunny looks at Ahmaad and throws the pissy pregnancy test in his face with as much force as she could muster, "Ouch!". She storms out of the bathroom and into her bedroom slamming the door behind her. She throws herself across the bed and cries into her pillow. She hears Ahmaad coming into the room.

"Sunny you can't be upset for me asking. I need to know. I know you went out with other guys but I don't know of anyone you fucked outside of Tyra. So what's good, keep it real with me." Sunny sits up and wipes her tears with the sleeve of her shirt. "No I never fucked another nigga. This is your fucking kid you asshole." "Okay I'm sorry. Now let's get an understanding.... Don't ever say you can't have my baby. You will not kill my child. We will do what we gotta do to take care of these kids. I will work my ass off to make sure y'all straight. So please don't ever let me hear you say that again... we understand each other?" "Understood, Ahmaad." "Now we have to make you a Doctor appointment and it's over for the drinking and smoking." "yeah well let's not forget we still not on good terms and we need to figure shit out. You have a whole baby with a bitch you cheated on me with. That's a huge fucking problem and I don't want you to think just because I'm pregnant I have to stay with your cheating ass. We got a lot of fucking issues on the floor Ahmaad and this baby is only going to add to it."

"I understand what you saying but I aint worried bout none of that. Do you realize when you told me you were pregnant with Caleb how devastating that was for me because I thought I would never be able to plant my seed in a woman. I went through some dark times. I thought my chance at having kids was taken from me when I was abused as a kid. It really fucked me up. And now I'm about to have my third baby! You have no idea how blessed I feel right now baby. I'm not worried about shit I know everything will work itself out."

"I'm glad you're so confident. So have you fucked your baby mama?" "Hell no. Not since you caught me. Now she's tried to come on to me like every time I come over but I've never even so much as kissed her." "I want her and the baby over here today. We need to have a conversation. All three of us." "I will do that Sunny. I told you anything I will do it's already done. Let me call her now."

10

A few hours later, Sunny is awakened by the doorbell. "I got it baby it's probably Veronica." Sunny springs up out the bed and gets herself together to face this bitch. She combs her hair and puts it in a high messy bun, put a lil lip gloss on, a shirt with a hi low rise affect. High in the front exposing her stomach and low in the back covering only half of her ass and she slipped some yoga pants on that shows off her camel toe. Ahmaad comes back into the room. "She out here bae." "Alright here I come." Sunny walks down the hallway and the first thing she sees is the baby car seat on the floor and tiny feet poking out of the front.

She can't seem to focus on anything except the baby. She walks closer and sees a miniature Ahmaad gnawing on his tiny baby fist. "He looks just like you Maad." Sunny says. She looks up and sees Veronica eyeballing her up and down with a scowl on her face. "So you called me over here so I'm here." Veronica says while chewing and popping her cum. Her body snapped right back and her jeans is showing off her coke bottle figure. She cut her hair into a pixie cut which aged her. She looks like a MILF now and not so much as a young hoe. "Yeah well thank you for bringing my son over. We need to talk to you V. Sunny is my wife and she's accepted Junior." Sunny interrupts…"He's named after you?" Sunny asks. Ahmaad grabs Sunny's hand, "Yes baby. Ahmaad the second. Sunny looks at Veronica as she sits on her couch smirking at her with one raised eyebrow. "Great name baby." Sunny leans in and kisses Ahmaad on the lips. Sunny looks back at Veronica with the same smirk she gave her. "So Veronica, Sunny is my sons step mother. She will be in his life no matter what and we just have to figure this shit out." The baby starts to whine. Veronica gets him out of his car seat and pulls her breast out to feed him. "Okay that's fine with me y'all just make sure my child support payments on time. Other than that I don't have shit else to say. That's y'all issue not mine. Just take care of my baby." Sunny is hella annoyed. "Veronica I know you can't help but be a bitch because you in love with my HUSBAND. But your son won't want for anything. And as far as you and I go, just don't be disrespectful and we won't have any problems. Can we agree on that?" "Yeah and the same goes for me Sunny." "And one more thing, stop throwing your pussy on my husband. That's disrespectful and if I find out it continues after this conversation then you and I will have a problem." Veronica laughs...."Maybe you should tell your husband to stop coming over my house with a hard on." Sunny grabs Ahmaad's dick through his grey jogging pants, showing off every inch of his erection. "Oh you mean like this? He can't help himself. His dick is a dick. It gets hard for just about anything. But just know my name is all over it. This is my dick." Sunny says while slow stroking Ahmaad's dick making him uncomfortable as his cheeks turn red. "Baby she knows whose dick this is. I tell her every time. She can't say that I haven't." Veronica is getting upset. She burps the baby and puts him back in his car seat as he drifts back off to sleep. "Y'all are some fucking weirdos and I got a man. Ahmaad like I said just have my money every week and we won't have no issues." "Veronica don't play me like a check book and don't disrespect me like I won't take care of my responsibilities. My job is to take care of him not you. Remember that shit." "Whatever the fuck. I'm sure you both heard what I said. We have to go." "You need some help?" Sunny asks Veronica. "Nah we straight." Veronica responds while rolling her eyes. Sunny chuckles to herself. Ahmaad picks up the carrier, "See you later daddy's man. Daddy loves you." Ahmaad says as he plants kisses on his son's cheeks. Veronica is obviously in her feelings as she stands at the door shaking her leg like she has a nervous tick. Ahmaad takes the baby outside to the car and Sunny watches his every move and Veronicas lips. "That was some hoe ass shit. I didn't appreciate all that extra bullshit." Veronica tells Ahmaad. "V, you gotta understand my wife's position. It's just something you gotta get over. And I want my son tomorrow." "Come and get him then." Veronica says. "Sunny will. Just make sure he has enough milk."

"No fuck that. She is not coming to my house to get my baby. Fuck that." Ahmaad looks at Veronica dead in her eyes. "You heard what the fuck I said. Don't play with me. She'll be there tomorrow at 1. See you tomorrow daddy's man." "I can't fucking stand you. I hope you know you married a hoe. Fuck the both of y'all and tell her to bring my money tomorrow too!" Veronica shouts. "Yeah, whatever." Ahmaad shuts the car door and heads in the house as Veronica burns rubber down the street. "Stupid ass bitch." Ahmaad mumbles. "So how much u been giving this hoe?" Sunny asks her husband. "No set amount. Just whatever she been saying she need. It was $100 last week." "Yeah well that's gone change. You need to give her a set amount because she's just going to use that baby to extort money out of us. I know you don't want no papers on you but you just have to do it. You can't give hoes like her the benefit. Plus, you got connections downtown so you know what to do." Sunny schools her husband. "Alright bae, first thing Monday I'll going to FOC. I told her you were picking up junior tomorrow around 1. Is that okay with you?" "Yeah I don't give a fuck about that bitch. I'll go get him." Ahmaad walks over to Sunny and picks her up off her feet and wraps her legs around his waist. "How did I get so lucky?" Ahmaad says. "Yeah well don't feel to lucky because I'm still not feeling you." "I know baby. Kiss me." Sunny softens and leans down to kiss her husband. He slid his tongue in-between her plump supple lips. She tasted the pineapples and watermelon he ate for breakfast on his tongue. He tastes so sweet and his lips are sending shock waves thru her body. "Ok put me down. I'm not fucking with you Ahmaad." Sunny says while trying to suppress her smile. "You such a hard ass. Alright baby. Alright. Fuck, I love you." Ahmaad says while putting Sunny down. "You better."

Sunny wakes up early the next day and felt like making her Husband breakfast before he went to work. He held her the entire night and didn't try anything sexual. He just wanted her close to him. Anytime she moved he moved with her. She felt the connection between them repairing itself and strengthening. Despite everything she's done, he loves her still and wants to work on their marriage. She's starting to feel the same and she even caught herself rubbing her belly at the thought of their baby growing inside her. "Oh damn it smells good as fuck in here. I get breakfast this morning? You sending me off to work right baby. Thank you." Ahmaad says as he ties his tie and tucks his shirt in his trousers.

"Yeah, I felt like cooking this morning. And last

night was really nice. I've missed you Ahmaad. I've missed us. I want us to work. In spite of everything. I need you." Ahmaad walks over to Sunny, grabs her face and kisses her passionately. "I love you so much Sunny. I vow to never break our vows again. Never. I love you too much to hurt you like this again. I aint worth shit without you." He kisses his wife again. "You really aint. Now shit your ass down while I make your plate. I don't want you late and you're not eating in your car." "Yes ma'am." Sunny made chicken and waffles with strawberry syrup. Sunny side up eggs and a bowl of grits with salt and pepper. Just the way he likes it. Ahmaad ate like he hasn't had a meal in over a week. The food didn't last on his plate ten minutes. "Damn I don't wanna go to work now. I need a nap ha-ha." "You better take your ass to work with all these kids running around here."

Sunny says as she walks over to him and unzips

his slacks. “Now that your belly is full I want your nuts empty.” Sunny says seductively while staring intensely into Ahmaad’s eyes. “Yes ma’am” Ahmaad lays back in the kitchen stool as Sunny takes his dick and balls out of his boxers and rest them against the waist band. “Dick stay hard. Damn I missed sucking your dick.” Sunny says right before she gobbles Ahmaad’s dick in one swift motion. She deep throats his steel pole off the first head bob. She slides the shaft out her throat slowly until she gets middle way and she deep throats again. Using short swift motions as the head of his dick hits the back of her throat causing saliva to build up in her mouth. Her juices cover Ahmaad’s dick and starts sliding down his balls. “I love my wife. I fucking love my wiiiife!” Ahmaad moans out in ecstasy. “Take this shit off!” Sunny demands Ahmaad to remove his pants. He quickly slides them down to his ankles. “Stand up”

Ahmaad does exactly what Sunny says. Sunny stands up and walks around Ahmaad facing his back. She reaches in front of him and starts stroking his dick. Spreading her spit all over his Johnson. She kneels down and starts kissing his ass cheeks. He clinches. She kisses more and more. Getting closer to his ass crack. He clinches even more. She takes her hand in between his legs and jerks his dick and she buries her face in between his ass, rimming his asshole. Ahmaad stumbles almost losing his balance. He holds onto the refrigerator. Sunny doesn't miss a stroke or a lick. She makes moaning and sucking noises like she's eating steak. His dick feels like a steel flag pole in her hands. She feels the base of his dick pulsating. He's about to blow. Sunny tongue fucks her husband's ass. He leans onto the refrigerator and holds on for dear life as his seed splatters against the fridge door. "Ahhhhhhh!

Fuuuuuuccccckkkkk!!!!" Ahmaad screams out.

Sunny eases up and plants small kisses on his asshole then his ass cheeks. She stands up and tells him, "Don't move." "Shit, how?" Ahmaad says. Sunny bust out laughing. She runs to the bathroom and gets a warm soapy washcloth and a dry washcloth. She Cleans all her DNA off his ass and balls. Ahmaad can't stop staring at her. She pulls his boxers up then his slacks. Zips him back up, buttons and buckles his slacks and belt. Straightens his tie and kisses him on the cheek, "Have a great day today, husband." "I will. Got damn I will. You see why I'm so fucking crazy over you? You do shit like this and expect me just to act normal? Nah fam. Nah." "Nigga take your ass to work before you're late." Sunny says while giggling. "Alright, laters mama." Ahmaad says while kissing Sunny as he heads out the door.

Sunny gets herself showered and dressed for

work. She's feeling optimistic about her marriage, this new life growing inside of her and the decision to end her friendship with Tyra and anyone else she deemed toxic. Today she was assigned to cashier for her shift. "This is going to be a long ass day. I'd prefer stock but whatever. Let's get it." She thought to herself after her manager gave her the assignment. It was a slow day. Sunny occupied herself by doing crossword puzzles on the side of her register inconspicuously. "I need assistance, now!" says an irate customer at Sunny's lane. Sunny looks up and see's it's Shalisha and Tyra. Sunny's blood started to boil. Her facial expression morphed into something angry, dark and very sinister. Her brows furrowed and her cheeks were flushed. Sweat started to form on her forehead. Her hands trembled. She envisioned herself grabbing Shalisha by her hair and banging her head into her cash register over and over and over. Her eyes were locked on her Shalisha. Hoping she felt froggy enough to leap.

"Yeah you're gonna need assistance alright. The fuck you wanna do?" Sunny says to Shalisha. "Sunny just ring up this shit. Don't do nothing stupid to risk your job." Tyra says. "Shut up, Bitch. Nobody asked you shit. You sit there and keep your mouth shut." Sunny says to Tyra while pointing her finger in her face but never breaking eye contact with Shalisha. "So what's up bitch? What you wanna do?" Sunny asks Shalisha. "I want you to be a good lil cashier and ring my shit up. Do your job." Shalisha says with her arms folded under her breast. Making sure her left hand sat on top to show off her wedding ring. "I've waited a long fucking time for this moment." *Ptooie* Sunny spits in Shalisha's face. "You fucking bitch! I'm going to kill you!" Shalisha screams as she lunges across the conveyer belt and grabs a hold of Sunny's

Home Depot Apron.

Sunny grabs two fists full of Shalisha's hair and yanks her down on the ground. Sunny straddles Shalisha and delivers powerful blows to her face over and over and over again. Causing blood to squirt all over her apron. Tyra runs around the cash register and attempts to pull Sunny off Shalisha. Sunny flung her head back with as much force as she could muster and the back of her head hit Tyra dead in her face. Tyra covers her mouth as blood drips from her lips. The manager, two stockers and a loss prevention undercover guard ran over to the commotion. It took all of them to pull Sunny off Shalisha. She was bucking and salivating like a rabid dog. "Take her in the back! Get her out of here!" Sunny's manager screams. The three associates struggle to get Sunny in the back loading dock area, but they managed with her bucking and clawing the entire way.

She finally started to calm down once back on the dock. "Damn girl. What the fuck did she do to you?" The undo asks. "Threatened my life. That's what she did." Sunny says while struggling to find her breath. "Just chill and have a seat. You gonna be here for a while. You know they calling the police."

"Yeah…whatever. I need my purse and my phone. I need to call my husband before they take me in." The stock boy who Sunny smokes weed with on their breaks agreed to go get her belongings. Sunny is finally calm and she looks herself over. She broke 4 nails, two of which broke from the nail bed, and her right hand was swollen twice its size. Her coworker came back with her belongings and she grabbed her phone and called Ahmaad immediately. He didn't answer. She calls him again. No answer. She calls a third time and leaves a message.

"Why aren't you answering your phone? Look I may be in jail by the time you get this. Shalisha and Tyra came up to my job and we got into a fight. Call me or my manager if I don't answer. Bye." Sunny puts her phone in her back pocket. The docking doors open and she hears walkie talkies and keys jiggling. It's Calvin, in full uniform with a matching blue/black eye. Sunny looks confused. She doesn't understand why he's the responding officer when she assumed he worked for a Detroit district. She starts thinking a little deeper and puts two and two together. The way they met was a set up. Maad set her up to meet Calvin downtown asleep in her car because he had been following her for however long already. "Sunny you just can't seem to stay clear of trouble." Officer Calvin says. "By the looks of your face, neither can you." Sunny says boldly. Calvin is pissed. "I need you to put your hands behind your back ma'am. Now!"

Sunny says nothing.

She rolls her eyes and turns around with her hands behind her back, ready to be cuffed. “You have the right to remain silent. Anything you say can and will be used against you in the court of law. I suggest you shut the fuck up...ma’am.” Calvin says as he tightens the cuffs on Sunny’s wrist. Calvin walks Sunny through the store and to his squad car. All eyes were on Sunny and she held her head high. Keeping her cool and composure. “You know you sent that girl to the hospital by ambulance. You could be looking at attempted murder. She lost consciousness.” Calvin says. “Is that right.” Sunny responds. “Watch your head.” Calvin says as he pushes Sunny into the back seat. Sunny stumbles inside the backseat, falling over on her side. Calvin gets in the car and cuts off his radio.

“So did you call your husband?” Calvin asks. “Of

"The train station? Why are we at the abandoned train station downtown?" Sunny made sure to say the location loud hoping the operator was still on the call. Calvin gets out of the car. He takes his gun out of the holster and cocks the barrel, putting one in the chamber. Sunny starts shaking. He walks over to Sunny's door and grabs her arm. Pulling her out of the car. He un-cuffs her. "Sunny I don't want to hurt you so please don't make me. Your husband has to pay for what he's done. There's no way around it. Just do what I tell you to do and you can escape this unscathed. Understood?" Sunny shakes her head yes with tears welling up in her eyes. Calvin holds onto Sunny's elbow with a firm grip to ensure she won't snatch away from him. They enter into the train station through the front doors. They were heavy and squeaky upon touch. "Ahmaad!!!!" Sunny screams as she sees Ahmaad sitting in a chair, unconscious and bleeding from his mouth and ears.

Sunny runs over to him and tries to assess him. “Maad baby? Baby get up! Get up baby!” “He can’t hear you.” Sunny stood straight up. She felt like jumping out of her skin. This voice sent chills down her spine and the little hairs on the back of her neck stood straight up. “Ezra? What the fuck? How the fuck? What the fuck? You muthafucka!!!!!!!” Sunny lunges after Ezra and knocks his glasses off his face. Just before she could claw his eyes out, Calvin grabbed her by her waist. “Whoa whoa whoa cow girl! Calm down now! Whoa!” Calvin says. “How the fuck did he get out? What the fuck are you doing this for Calvin? Why? Why he here?” “He’s here to execute some street justice. He stole you from this man and in turn made him lose his fucking mind. He then, assaults me and make up lies trying to ruin my career because I fell for you and I tried to lookout for you.

He must know what he did wrong and can't ever do it again." Calvin says. "You're both going to jail for life, muthafuckas!! You can't do this! You can't do this!" Sunny screams. Calvin pushes her down and makes her sit on the bench. "Go get that water." Calvin orders Ezra. Ezra grabs a bucket of water from the corner of the train station. Being careful not to spill it. He douses Ahmaad with the bucket of ice cold water. Ahmaad is awakened. He's shaken up but he's awake. "Sunny" Ahmaad tries to focus his eyes on Sunny but can't see through the blood. "I'm here baby. I'm here. Hold on Maad. Don't you leave me! Calvin please let him go I'm pregnant! We're expecting another baby and I don't want to raise another child without it's father! Please!" *POW* Ezra punches Ahmaad in the face. Causing his head to fly back so forcefully he fell out of the chair. Ahmaad spits blood and pieces of his teeth out onto the cold dirty cracked cemented floor.

"Nigga, you hit like a bitch. Untie me bitch and let's go head up!" Ezra kicks Ahmaad in his face knocking him out cold. Ezra starts stomping on his ribs and hips. "Chill out! Chill! I don't want him to die yet young blood. Stop!" Calvin yells out to Ezra, commanding him to stop but Ezra doesn't listen. He keeps beating Ahmaad and looking at Sunny the entire time. Sunny is screaming hysterically. "Do something!! Do something! He's going to kill him!!" Ahmaad's body starts to convulse violently. A mixture of foam and blood pours from his mouth. Calvin looks as if he's in shock yet enjoying watching Ahmaad die slowly. Sunny grabs Calvin's gun out his holster, *BAM* one shot into Calvin's belly. The sound of the gun startled Ezra as he stumbled and fell on his backside. Sunny struggled to cock the gun again but remembers it's a semi-automatic and all she has to do is squeeze the trigger until it's empty.

"Get the fuck away from him you sick piece of shit! Get away from him before I blow your fucking head off!" Ezra puts his hands up above his head and slowly starts inching his way over to Sunny. "You don't want to kill me Sunny. I love you and you still love me. This nigga is in the way. Nobody will ever love you the way I do. Don't you know that? He can't make you cum like I can. He doesn't make you feel the way I make you feel. Don't you see he's just a temp? He's not permanent. Now put that gun away and let's get out of here. Sunny is trembling in fear. She can barely see through her tears. "Get back! Get the fuck back! Don't you come any clo…" Ezra grabs the gun and throws it. He puts Sunny in the choke hold. "Take me to the fucking car bi…"

"FREEZE!! Let her go or we will shoot you! Let her go and put your hands up!" Detroit police

Department stormed the train station. 20 police officers had their weapons drawn, aimed and ready to fire. “You don’t want to do this buddy; it’s going to end bad for you. Let the lady go!” DPD negotiator says. “It’s already bad for me!” Ezra says. He puts his hands on Sunny’s head trying to snap her neck, *PEW PEW* Ezra’s body drops to the floor hard. A sniper in the stained window put two in his head. Sunny faints.

“Push! You gotta push mama! Come on you can do this! Push!” Veronica coaches Sunny as she gives birth to her miracle baby. “I can’t! She won’t come out! I don’t want to do this! Nooooooooo Ahhhhhhhhhhh Grrrrrrrrr!” Sunny crowns. Her mom and stepdad take pictures. Her stepdad is so overwhelmed he starts crying. “You doing it baby girl! Linda she doing it!” Sunny’s stepdad rejoices.

waaaaaaaaaaa waaaaaaaaaaaa “It's a girl!!” Everyone screams.

Sunny cries uncontrollably as they place her baby on her breast. “My baby girl! My baby girl! Thank you God! Thank you!” Sunny cries out in elation. “Mommy you did it. She looks just like Ahmaad. She's so beautiful mommy. I'm so proud of you.” Veronica says as she kisses Sunny on her forehead. The two became really close since Ahmaad's been in a coma. Veronica has been by Sunny's side everyday helping her with anything she needed, even going to her doctor's appointments. It's as if they became sister wives. The only thing she didn't help with is the care of Ahmaad. Sunny wanted to care for him herself. She goes to see him every day. She reads to him, baths him and exercises his limbs. She's never missed a day until today to give birth to their daughter. The doctors diagnosed Ahmaad as brain dead, but Sunny refused to pull the plug until He met his daughter.

Sunny had an influx of visitors all day. She finally asked the nurses to refuse anymore visitors. It was time for Ahmaad to meet his daughter, Hamda. The nurses wheeled Sunny to Ahmaad's room with baby Hamda. Sunny was overcome by emotions. She asked the nurse to hold her baby so she could climb in the bed and lay with Ahmaad for the last time. "Hi my love. She's here. She's finally here. I named her Hamda. I knew you wouldn't have it any other way. My love. My dear heart. I love you so much. You've given me so much joy so much love. My heart is so full Ahmaad. You've done your job. I prayed and prayed ever since I was a little broken girl for someone to come into my life and love me. Love me unconditionally. Love me the way love is supposed to love. You've done your job. And now your love will live through our children. And I am forever grateful. I love you with everything I am dear heart."

Sunny kisses Ahmaad on his cheek and holds him tightly. Tubes are running out his mouth, breathing for him. "Nurse, my baby please." The nurse, who is crying herself passes the baby to Sunny. "Here she is Ahmaad. Your daughter. Princess Hamad." Sunny lays the baby on Ahmaad's chest. She asks the nurse to take pictures. Sunny is so strong so courageous. The nurse keeps clicking. She wants to take as many pictures as she can. Sunny just lays with her husband and baby, soaking up every moment, every memory.

"Sunny!! His eyes are open!! Holy shit!" The nurse shouts. Sunny sits up so fast she got dizzy! Ahmaad was looking at his daughter! The nurse ran out in the hall and called the doctors into the room. The doctors asked Sunny to take the baby so they could assess

Ahmaad. Sunny refused to leave the room. She, baby and nurse remained quietly tucked in the corner praying incessantly. “Let’s extubate him.” The doctors pulled the tube out of Ahmaad’s throat. He coughed and coughed for what seemed an eternity. Sunny was so afraid. Finally, he stopped. “Where’s my wife and daughter?” Ahmaad asked. “Here we are baby! We’re right here my love! Thank you father God! Thank you for finally shinning your light on me!

www.ingramcontent.com/pod-product-compliance
Lightning Source LLC
Chambersburg PA
CBHW030243030726
47493CB00023B/565

* 9 7 8 0 6 9 2 8 7 6 9 0 9 *